Stay Seek'n magical [handwritten]

JAGGER JONES
& THE MUMMY'S ANKH

MALAYNA EVANS

TANTRUM BOOKS

Month9Books

This book is a work of fiction. Names, characters, places, and incidents are either products of the author's imagination or are used fictitiously. Any resemblance to actual persons, living or dead, business establishments, events, or locales is entirely coincidental. The author makes no claims to, but instead acknowledges the trademarked status and trademark owners of the word marks mentioned in this work of fiction.

Copyright © 2019 by Malayna Evans

JAGGER JONES & THE MUMMY'S ANKH by Malayna Evans
All rights reserved. Published in the United States of America by Month9Books, LLC. No part of this book may be used or reproduced in any manner whatsoever without written permission of the publisher, except in the case of brief quotations embodied in critical articles and reviews.

Trade Paperback ISBN: 978-1-948671-62-0
ePub ISBN: 978-1-948671-63-7
Mobipocket ISBN: 978-1-948671-64-4

Published by Tantrum Books for Month9Books, Raleigh, NC 27609
Cover Design by Danielle Doolittle
Cover Illustration by Tatiana A. Makeeva

To my muse, Gracian

JAGGER JONES
& THE MUMMY'S ANKH

IN DE NILE

"What's she doing now?" Jagger moaned as his little sister spun and zoomed back into the house.

"Don't leave without me," Aria yelled. She whizzed through the front door held open by Grams, who lived in the other side of their red brick, two-flat with Gramps.

"Grabbing Jerry?" Mom guessed.

"Is Jerry the stuffed yellow pig or the orange zebra?" He leaned back against the yellow cab that was waiting to take him, Mom and Aria to the airport. Again.

"Jerry is the pink mouse."

He almost asked why the pink mouse wasn't a girl, but he'd heard Mom's lectures on gender constructs enough times to give them himself. Besides, Jagger would be perfectly happy to miss their plane. Crisscrossing the planet was Mom's thing … and Aria's. Jagger just wanted to stay home and enroll in Chicago's most selective middle school with his best friend, Andrew. But because of Mom's travel-writer job, he and Aria were homeschooled from around the globe: Singapore, Sydney, Samoa. He once wrote a history paper from a lodge in Senegal.

"Let's go," Aria howled as she ran out of the house, kissed Grams' wrinkled cheek, then hiked her enormous, purple bag over her shoulder and rushed to the cab. Her dark, blond curls bounced, framing her face like a mane.

She didn't have Jerry, just her over-sized, sparkly purse. On the bright side, if Jagger needed a snack, or a charger, or, possibly, a pet zebra on their zillion-hour flight, there was a good chance Aria could mine it from the depths of her bag.

"She's trading toys for fashion," Mom joked, waving goodbye to Grams one last time. "Our baby is growing up."

Jagger cringed. He hated it when Mom referred to Aria as *their* baby. His sister was eleven-years-old, just two years younger than him. But Mom sometimes acted like Jagger was her co-parent. Her mantra was: *it's your job to take care of your sister*. So Jagger watched after Aria, and his aging grandparents, alone, while Mom travelled the world to put a roof over their heads.

The only thing worse than being forced to play grown-up was being dragged from one exotic locale to another.

Stifling an eye roll, Jagger slid in next to Aria, who was perched in the middle of the cab's back seat, arms wrapped around her precious purple cargo.

"You must be excited, Brainy." Aria always called him Brainy. Jagger took it as a compliment: he *was* smarter than her, after all.

"About what? Spending the next twenty-four hours in planes and airports and cabs? Or teaching you math at forty thousand feet?"

Mom gave the cabbie instructions as Aria flashed the silver-haired stranger her you'd-love-me-if-you-knew-me grin. She turned to Jagger. "We're going to your favorite place, right?"

"And not just to Egypt," Mom chimed in before Jagger could respond. "We're going to Amarna, Egypt, where the fanatic pharaoh you're so interested in once ruled."

"It's not like he's going to be there," Jagger sighed.

"Yeah, but I thought you said the Amar-uh Time was the greatest period in history."

"The Uh-mar-na Period," Jagger corrected his sister, articulating each syllable slowly so she could wrap her little brain around the word.

Aria didn't stifle *her* eye roll—she just let it fly.

"And it *was* the coolest period ever," he added. "I'd just rather read about it, in my room, with a big bag of chips, than stare at old rocks left behind by people who died thousands of years ago."

"Maybe you can read *next* to the rocks." Mom smoothed a stray black curl back into the ponytail at the nape of her neck. "We'll call it Adventure Reading."

Aria laughed. "It's like Adventure Eating, but for nerds!"

Jagger ignored them, staring out the window as Mom and Aria made more 'adventure' jokes. The two of them shared the irrational belief that adding the word 'adventure' before a thing magically rendered it more interesting. Aria loved things like Adventure Eating—eating food no one you knew had ever eaten before. Jagger, on the other hand, spent their days abroad longing for hamburgers and deep-dish pizza.

The cab turned onto Lake Shore Drive from their South Side neighborhood, which was stuffed with small bungalows and two-flats and mom-and-pop shops. The city stretched tall in the distance. Lake Michigan looked extra blue in the morning light. It changed colors depending on algae and nutrients. And mussels, which made the lake prettier, but also led to less phytoplankton, which meant fewer fish. That was bad for fishermen like Gramps, a retired military vet who spent his free hours with a pole in his hand.

Jagger watched the lake fly past in a blur of blue and green until the cab rolled to a stop at a red light. He flinched, startled by a huge, black cat that jumped onto the railing separating the street from the park, running miles along the lake, teeming with bikers and dog walkers. The cat stared at Jagger with shrewd, green eyes, like it was judging him. It was so close Jagger could pet it if he rolled down the window.

Jagger kept his eyes on the uncanny cat until the cab rushed forward, then he shook himself: *cats don't size up thirteen-year-old boys.*

"Traffic is light today," the cabbie said in an accent Jagger recognized as East End London ... because of course they'd spent a week in London last year. "We should be at O'Hare in less than an hour."

Jagger's eyes snapped open. He sat up and sucked in a ragged breath. Sweat trickled down his back as he searched the one-room rental house for the voice that had called his name.

"A dream," he muttered, laying back down and rolling onto his side to stare at his mom and little sister, asleep in the other bed. He yanked the sheet over his head, trying to ignore the familiar anger bubbling up, lodging in his throat like a wad of three-day-old gum—anger over their chaotic life of travel and instability. Sure they were in the one place on Earth Jagger would want to see *if* he were the type of historian who wanted to *see* the places he read about. But he wasn't!

Meow.

The black cat Aria had caught moments after their tiny plane landed in Amarna pawed at him. Jagger lowered the sheet and watched it flick its tail back and forth, then jump to the other bed and snuggle next to Aria. His sister had a knack for adopting strays and for acting hysterical when Mom made her leave them all behind.

It blinked its eerily familiar green eyes, then licked its paws and ignored him.

Jagger Jones!

"Ah!" Jagger shot out of bed. He grabbed his phone from the nightstand and shined its LED light around the room, heart hammering in his chest. "Who's there?"

Come, Jagger Jones!

Okay. Not a dream. The voice came from outside. It sounded like a girl. But he didn't know any Egyptian girls. He didn't know anyone in Amarna. This could *not* be real.

Jagger Jones!

Slipping on his high tops, Jagger tiptoed across the room. He glanced over at Mom. She breathed heavily through parted lips, but she didn't budge. He paused at the door, his sweaty hand on the knob. Maybe he was still asleep. Or maybe the heat was getting to him. Or perhaps his topsy-turvy family life had finally pushed him over the edge.

Jagger Jones!

Or, maybe, some girl really was outside, calling his name.

With a backward glance, Jagger unbolted the door and peeked out. No girl, just archeological ruins, ringed by limestone cliffs. The Nile River flowed serenely past, creating a natural border on one side. The Egyptian, night sky was brilliant, with stars so big and heavy he felt like he could reach out and touch them.

Come, Jagger Jones!

"Hello?" Jagger whispered as he stepped out, shutting the door gently behind him. Pink gravel crunched under his favorite shoes as he threaded his way through the small, scattered, mud-brick houses that belonged to locals who farmed the nearby fields and rented their homes to scholars and archeologists and stalwart adventurers like his mom.

He rubbed his arms—the wind was chilly—and cursed himself silently. He knew better than to venture off alone into a foreign desert as surely as he knew the square root of pi, the circumference of the sun, and the inauguration date of every American president. But his big brain couldn't stop his dumb body from moving forward—he *had* to find this girl.

Jagger Jones!

She must be just ahead, close to the cliff face. Was she pranking him? Who was she? How was she throwing her voice like that? An app, maybe? Some kind of AI? A new spin on voice verification? And how did she know his name?

BBBBZZZZZZZZZZ.

7

Jagger jumped. Heart racing, he glanced at his buzzing phone's screen. Five old texts from Andrew and a new one from Dad showed on the screen. At least it wasn't Mom, busting him. His best friend had texted him hours earlier. Dad, on the other hand, was texting in the middle of the night, Amarna time. Because of course he was. Dad never thought of anyone but himself—it wouldn't dawn on him that the timing was inconvenient for Jagger. Worse, Dad would be mad if Jagger didn't respond immediately, as if a guy who refused to spend time with Jagger and Aria, or help pay for them, deserved a midnight reply!

Jagger Jones!

The voice reclaimed his attention. It sounded muffled now, like it was coming from under his feet. She couldn't be underground. Could she? Jagger shoved his phone in his pocket and dropped to his knees, pressing his ear against the desert floor.

Jagger Jones! Come!

Yep. She was down there. But how?

He blew a puff of air, staring at his hands, resting on the red-tinted dirt. When the voice called out to him again, Jagger did the only thing he could think to do: he dug. The sand was hard. It squirmed underneath his nails, piercing him.

"Jagger! What are you doing?"

He scrabbled backward, startled by the familiar voice, invading his thoughts in that uncanny way of hers.

"Aria!" His voice was shrill.

His little sister hiked her purse onto her shoulder and stomped toward him, dust swirling at her feet. She was wheezing. Her asthma must be kicking in.

"You need—"

Aria held up one hand, as she pulled an inhaler—bejeweled, of course—from her purse with the other hand. After a few quick puffs, she asked again. "Seriously. What are you doing?"

"You need to go back," Jagger said.

Actually, they *both* needed to go back. Mom would ground him for life if something happened to Aria because she followed him on a midnight stroll through an Egyptian desert.

"Stop parenting me! I'm not a baby."

Jagger Jones!

"Did you hear that?" Jagger leaned forward, pressing his hands against the shifted dirt.

"Hear what? What are you talking about? Mom is going to—"

"Shhhh." His finger flew to his lips. "Listen."

Come, Jagger Jones!

Jagger studied his sister. Aria stood, hands on her hips, tapping one foot as she glared at him. She didn't react to the voice. She couldn't hear it.

Part relieved and part disappointed, Jagger snapped at

9

her, "This is none of your business, lil' sis. Go back before Mom wakes up and freaks out."

"And what am I supposed to say when she asks where you are? I mean, I know you have some crazy connection to this place, but really, I don't understand what's happening right now. You're usually so … so … boring!"

Jagger rolled his eyes. He knew she was right. He also knew from years of trying to ditch her that Aria wasn't going anywhere until she wanted to. "I'm …" He paused, feeling stupid. "I'm digging. Okay?"

Aria cocked her head to the side, then shrugged. Unlike Jagger, who liked things neat and tidy and sensical, Aria embraced a carefree worldview: anything was game as long as it seemed fun. "Okay. But, uh, shouldn't you use a shovel for that?"

"You think?" He rubbed his brow. "Do *you* have one handy?"

She tapped a finger against her cheek, then dropped to the ground and dug through her purse. She pulled out a small, orange bag with a ballerina bulldog on it. Unzipping it, she handed Jagger a pair of nail trimming scissors. A second later, she banged the ground where Jagger had been digging with an oversized, rainbow-colored pen.

"Really? You're just going to help me dig? This doesn't seem, you know, odd to you?"

Aria flashed him a bright smile. "Brainy, I'm happy

you're finally doing something interesting … as long as Mom doesn't find out!"

Come, Jagger Jones! Come!

The voice pulled Jagger's attention back to the desert floor. With Aria and her supplies, the digging went faster. Five minutes later, they broke the hard, top surface, and sand tumbled away, cascading down as if the Earth was inhaling, sucking it in.

Jagger's heart banged against his chest as he struggled to process what he saw.

"No. Way!" He breathed. "This *cannot* be happening!"

2

I WANT MY MUMMY!

Jagger stared, mouth agape, at the stairs leading down into the desert.

Had they just discovered a tomb?

He closed his eyes, counted to ten, then looked again.

The stairs were still there.

Jagger felt breathless. While other boys grew up fantasizing about playing pro football or flying a fighter jet, Jagger had dreamt of discovering an Egyptian tomb. But he didn't imagine discovering it in the middle of the night, on a trip with his mom and sister, by following a disembodied voice.

"What is it?" Aria brushed sand off the top step.

"I think it's a ... a ... tomb," Jagger stuttered. "But I know every tomb on the archeological maps, and there's not supposed to be one here."

"Then how did you know to dig here?"

That was a good question. Jagger shook his head, unsure of the answer.

Come, Jagger Jones!

Mystery Girl was definitely down there.

Aria bounced a pink sneaker on the top step, testing its strength. She never could resist anything with a whiff of adventure. Assured it would hold her weight, she donned an impish grin and crept down the crumbling, old steps, into the dark, foreboding tomb.

"Aria!" Jagger knew he should stop her.

Aria paused at the bottom and peered back up at him, her sandy-brown skin lit by starlight. Unlike Jagger, whose skin tone was more like Mom's, Aria took after Dad. She even had the same inquisitive, hazel eyes. She plugged her nose with one hand and pushed a few giant, kinky curls out of her face with the other.

Jagger's stomach squirmed as he looked at her. His rash act had put his sister in danger. He was breaking Mom's cardinal rule. But what was he supposed to do? Just walk away and forget a voice was summoning him from underground and that his sister was halfway down a mysterious flight of stairs that seemingly led to the voice ... and to an undiscovered tomb?

Come, Jagger Jones!

Jagger bit his lip, hard, then followed his sister down, pulling out his phone and selecting the flashlight app. The smell of old, sweaty socks hit him as he descended and slipped past Aria into the narrow hallway that stretched behind her, shining his light onto the walls. They were covered, floor to ceiling, in artwork. Brilliant, awesome, incredible artwork.

"What's that?" Aria pointed at the strange character illuminated by Jagger's phone.

"It's not a what. It's a who," he breathed. "That's Egypt's fanatical pharaoh, Akhenaten." Jagger spotlighted the figure etched deeply into the bedrock as he ran his hand over it, entranced by the grooves some artist had carved thousands of years ago. Art from the Amarna period was completely different from the predictable look of Egyptian art from all other periods, like a colorful cubist painting stuck in a gallery of black and white photographs.

Akhenaten, tall and gangly with an egg-shaped head and a bare belly bulging over his kilt, stared down at them. He wore a towering, rounded hat and a gaudy necklace. Four women lined up behind him. The queen was nearly as tall, with a transparent dress that revealed her arms and legs. Three princesses followed her, all wearing chunky necklaces like their dad's and all bald but for ponytails that stuck out on the side of each girl's head.

"Why are you so interested in him?" Aria asked, staring up at the image. "I mean, there were loads of pharaohs.

What's so special about him?"

"Lots of things," Jagger said as he moved the light up, and inched forward. "Including this guy here. He's the royal family's sun god." A giant sun disk dominated much of the wall. Its rays ended in claw-like hands that reached toward the family members, looking as though it wanted to pat them on the head, or, more ominously, catch them in its claws like toys in some vintage, arcade game.

"That's a god? I thought Egyptian gods were people with animal heads." Aria reached out, and placed both palms against the etched rock.

"You need to pay more attention in social studies. Egyptian gods—"

Jagger Jones! Come!

Jagger pivoted toward the voice. He wiped his sweaty hands on his pants, glancing at Aria. No reaction. But he *couldn't* be imagining it. His imagination couldn't have led him to a buried tomb! He aimed his flashlight down the hall, feeling jingly, like he'd just stuck his finger in an outlet.

Aria nudged him, and he moved forward, holding his phone in one hand and pulling his sister with the other. Tomb discovery was equal parts thrilling and terrifying; he wanted her close. The air grew staler as they crept farther down the hall.

"Noooo!" Jagger moaned when his phone's flashlight illuminated a problem about fifteen feet in.

A giant boulder blocked the hallway.

He banged his hand against the oversized rock, his stomach churning with disappointment.

Jagger Jones!

She was on the other side. She must be in the tomb chamber. The mere thought of an undiscovered tomb chamber sent his pulse racing. Bracing his back against the wall, Jagger tried shoving the boulder to one side, and then the other. The rock wouldn't budge.

"Open already!" he muttered. He needed to get into the room that lay beyond this stupid rock.

Aria flashed him her you're-annoying-but-I-feel-sorry-for-you face. "Let's go get Mom." She yanked on his sweaty T-shirt, then grimaced and wiped her hands on her leopard-print leggings.

He really must have been losing his mind if Aria sounded like the rational one. Still, he wasn't ready to admit defeat. He'd have to take Aria back to Mom then return alone. He sighed. Resolved, he turned to light their way out, anxious to lose his sister so he could figure out how to get into the tomb chamber without the distraction of Aria buzzing around him.

Jagger Jones!

Jagger turned back to give the boulder one last glance. "Whoa!"

It had shifted, leaving a gap big enough for them to sneak through. Darkness poured out from the other side. The velvety darkness seemed tangible, like something one could touch and taste. It even *smelled* dark.

Jagger Jones! Come!

Her voice drifted out, oozing toward him like renegade smoke.

"Aria, do you see this?" He spun his sister around.

"Creepy." She budged closer to him. Then she leaned forward, drawn to the gloom. "Let's go in!"

Jagger held onto her, hesitating. He needed to keep going, but Aria should be back in the rental house with Mom.

"Come on." She yanked her arm, but he held her fast, weighing his options.

The urge to see what was in that room, to meet the girl who'd been calling out to him, was too strong to resist. He pushed Aria behind him, took a breath, and slipped past the rock, shining his flashlight around and gasping in awe.

The room glittered with gold. By some miracle, the tomb had escaped the notice of both ancient tomb robbers and modern scholars. He'd be a hero to geeks across the globe.

His breath quickened as he inched forward, trying not to step on any priceless objects. There was a chair with lion's paw feet, a gold chest, a broken chariot with gem-studded wheels, loads of gold and alabaster jugs, and more ancient knickknacks than his brain could process. Centuries of dust couldn't hide the beauty or fortune stuffed into this small room.

"Are we rich? We're rich, aren't we?" Aria exclaimed.

He ignored her, captivated by the open, stone box that stood at the far end of the room, flanked by two larger-than-life dog-headed statues. They were made of black stone and embossed with more gold. They gave him the heebie-jeebies. With a shiver, he shifted his attention back to the box. He knew it should contain a gold coffin built to house the tomb's mummy. He also knew the dog-headed guards couldn't possibly be watching him, but they felt alive, nonetheless.

"It moved!" Aria pointed. "Did you see that dog thing's eyes? They moved."

"It's a statue." He shifted closer to his sister. "It can't move."

"Maybe we should get Mom." Aria eyeballed the guards as if she expected them to wake up, and start searching for their next meal.

Jagger Jones!

The ghostly voice was coming from *inside* the stone box.

"One minute, lil' sis," he croaked. "I have to see the mummy."

"Just do what you have to do, and let's go. Mom is gonna kill us when she finds out we discovered a tomb while she was asleep. Maybe we should take this secret to *our* graves." Aria jabbered when she was anxious. "Think we can keep it secret and still get rich off it?" Her eyes darted from a gold chest to a gold chair. "Because this looks like a serious Michigan Avenue shopping spree ..."

Jagger tuned her out, holding his breath as he moved past the statues. He peered into the box, stomach churning. The lid lay on the ground by his feet. Surprisingly, the lid of the golden coffin nestled inside the box was gone too, leaving the mummy exposed. The bandages were intact and still clean; they covered every speck of the small body, too big to be a child but not quite an adult either.

"No way," he mumbled, staring at the large, gold amulet sitting on the mummy's belly. Jagger knew immediately that the amulet was the source of the mysterious voice. What he didn't know was how.

He gaped at the *ankh*, the Egyptian symbol of life, shaped like a cross with a loop at the top. The *ankh* was covered in gemstones that glimmered in the dim light. Something about the gemstones was off. They were transparent, more like holographic projections than real gemstones. And they seemed animated. Colorful lights rattled inside them, as if fireflies were trapped inside. But as unusual as they were, they couldn't explain the voice. Could they?

Wracking his brain for a scientific explanation, Jagger leaned in to get a better view of the fat, green chunk of malachite in the center of the *ankh*, bigger and sparklier than the other gemstones, just as Aria's hand reached for it.

He froze, terrified. He couldn't have said why, but he knew they shouldn't touch that thing.

"DON'T!"

His yell was drowned out by a strong wind that whirled, suddenly, around them. He grabbed his sister as a vortex formed. Colorful lights danced in the wind, as if they'd escaped from the gemstones.

"What's happening?" Aria clutched the amulet, eyes wide. "Let go of it!"

He didn't know if Aria didn't hear him, or if she was ignoring him. Either way, it was too late.

They *fell*!

Jagger reached for Aria's hand as their bodies spun, weightless, in empty space. Colorful lights swirled around them. The silence was deafening, even more profound after the voice had reverberated through his head for the past hour. Though Aria's mouth was open wide like she was screaming, he couldn't hear a thing.

With a sudden bump, Jagger felt the familiar comfort of solid ground beneath him as his stomach continued to tumble. Maybe he was sick, and this was all a dream. But how could that explain the plush carpet beneath him, or the bright light that streamed around him, or the unfamiliar smell wafting on the breeze that brushed his cheek?

Daring a panicked look around, Jagger gasped. "What the …"

"Breathe," Aria whispered. That's what Mom said when unexpected things happened.

But this wasn't unexpected. This was impossible!

A ROYAL SHOCK

They weren't in the tomb anymore.

And they weren't alone.

A girl, who looked a year or two older than Jagger, stood ten feet away, her back to a large, luxurious bed.

She was the fiercest looking girl Jagger had ever seen, and she was dressed in ancient Egyptian clothes like the ones he'd seen in history books. Her white, linen, shift dress fell to her knees. Golden sandals wound up her calves, and thick, gold bands circled her biceps like snakes. Her skin was a honey brown, like his, and she was bald. Well, not entirely bald. A thick, black ponytail made up of three fat braids hung down one side of her face like a lopsided curtain.

"Nice hairdo," Aria deadpanned.

"It means she's still a kid," he whispered back without looking at his sister. His eyes were stuck to the girl, but her background—a bedroom drenched in ancient Egyptian artifacts—was just as astonishing.

The girl shook her head, and the colorful amulets hanging from her braids jingled like armor. "How did *you* get here? Why do you look like …"? She bared her teeth. Was she angry? Her glare was aimed at Aria, as if thirteen-year-old boys fell out of the sky every day, but eleven-year-old girls were as unexpected as little, green aliens.

Jagger struggled to process the room. The wall beyond the bed was open to the outside. Columns, striped with bold bands of color, separated the internal space from the outdoors. He caught a glimpse of the Nile River flowing past, beyond palm trees that waved in the wind next to golden chairs with lion's paw feet. Inside, the room was stuffed with gold chests, alabaster vases, cedar chairs, and rich rugs. A blue ceiling with gold stars stretched over Jagger's head, and a painted fish poked its head out from the rug beneath his feet, as if it were swimming across the marble floor. The walls were painted with ancient Egyptian trees and animals; a blue goose flew across the wall above the girl's shoulder. The smell of cedar and cinnamon filled Jagger's nose, reminding him of Mom's favorite candle, mined from the shelves of an outdoor market in Bangkok.

The girl shifted her eyes from Aria to Jagger. "I cast the *Meseneh Rek* spell to summon *you,* Jagger Jones." She folded her arms and blew a puff of air. "I require your help." She was definitely the girl who'd been in his head. Her voice was low and musical. And familiar. "Whether you know it or not, you need mine too. We're both in grave danger."

Danger?

"We're in danger, because you kidnapped us!" Aria shot back. Jagger was too scared and confused to even make it to mad. What was going on here?

The girl scowled at Aria, as if his little sister was a dung beetle doing the backstroke through her favorite soup. "I don't know how *you* got here. I summoned only Jagger Jones." She lifted her chin. "And I assure you, the Princess of the Red and Black Land does *not* steal children. My family is in danger. And this boy shares our danger." She pointed a bejeweled finger at Jagger.

The Princess of the Red and Black Land?

Jagger knew that title. He knew that ancient Egyptians sometimes referred to their country as the "Red and Black Land."

"I don't care if you're Santa Claus," Aria retorted. "You've somehow brought us to this … this *place*. We're going to call our mom. And the police!"

The girl flashed a crooked smile, as if she felt genuinely sorry for the overwrought child before her. "If you're looking for authority figures, you've landed in the right place. I'm Princess Meretaten, eldest daughter of Pharaoh Akhenaten and

Queen Nefertiti, may they have life, prosperity, and health."

Meretaten? That name was familiar. He'd read about the royal princesses of Amarna. But she couldn't be *the* Meretaten. "What do you mean?" Jagger asked.

"Who cares what she means?" Aria rounded on him. "There has to be a trap door on the floor of that tomb. We need to get back. And we don't even know where we are!"

Jagger listened to his sister. He watched her mouth, focusing on the words. He imagined the letters hovering above her head in bold font. They were wrong somehow. Off. He closed his eyes, picturing the words as cryptograms. Cryptograms could be decoded. He just needed the cipher.

Red and Black Land.

Meretaten.

Velocity equals distance travelled divided by time.

He took a deep breath. Okay, so Einstein's theories about time travel must be right. But this? He opened his eyes. He couldn't believe the words he was about to utter.

"I don't think *where* we are is the problem." Jagger raised his voice to compete with the sound of his own heartbeat. He couldn't begin to calculate just how unlikely this was, and that was saying something—Jagger could calculate just about anything. "I think the problem is *when.*"

"*When?*" Aria stared at him like he was an eight-tentacled, flying octopus. But the girl gave him a solemn nod, as if Jagger was a pet that had just performed a clever trick.

"Yeah. *When.*"

Aria bit her lip, looking around like she expected an exit sign to flash on the wall next to one of the flying birds.

"Don't freak out," he continued. "Some legit scientific theories suggest time travel is possible. Even Einstein thought so. You've heard of Einstein, right?"

"Einstein? Seriously? We need to get you to a hospital!" Aria put her hand on Jagger's head like Grams did when checking for a fever. "Something's wrong with you. You don't believe in anything that's not science-y. And you think we've *travelled through time?*"

"Time travel *is* science-y, lil' sis." Jagger sounded calmer than he felt. "And this place is too authentic to be fake. Think about what's happened to us in the past hour. I followed a voice into the desert, and it led me to a tomb. You touched an amulet, and, bam! You felt that … *thing* that happened to us. And here we are. None of this makes sense. But the empirical evidence …"

Aria shook her head. She wasn't buying this.

Jagger sighed. Time to point out the pyramid-sized elephant in the room. "Some evidence can't be discounted. Think about the language you're using right now."

Aria crinkled her nose like she did when Grams tried to explain fractions.

The princess huffed. "We don't have time for this. We must proceed—"

"Wait!" Jagger interrupted her, sticking a hand out like a traffic cop before he turned back to Aria. "Okay. Let's try this. Repeat after me."

One eyebrow crawled up, but she didn't argue. With Aria, that was a win.

"I have the best big brother in the world."

She rolled her eyes but played along. "I have—"

"Think of the words you're saying."

"… the best …" Aria's hand flew to her mouth as she realized they were both speaking a language they'd never even heard before, a language no one had heard for centuries.

This fall back through time had gifted them with the ability to speak ancient Egyptian.

It was so natural he hadn't even noticed at first. Jagger had to admit, even Einstein, Stephen Hawking, and Marie Curie combined couldn't have come up with a scientific explanation for *that*.

Aria wound her fingers behind her neck and sucked in a few deep breaths. Then she shook her head and released a nervous giggle. "And you thought Mom's travel plans were bad! How far back are we?"

"About three thousand years," Jagger replied. He wanted to cry, but he felt like he should act tough for Aria's sake, which was ridiculous since they both knew she was tougher than him.

"Aaaaand we're still breathing," Aria said with a stupefied grin, before turning her attention to the girl. "Did she say her name was Merry Hot One?" she whispered to Jagger.

A sense of relief washed over him. Aria was always up for an adventure, but her tantrums were legendary. Happy she was going to hold it together, he whispered back, sounding out the princess's name: "Mare-et-ah-tun."

Aria put her hands on her hips and shook her head. "No. I just can't with that. I'm gonna call you ..." She stared at the ceiling. "Tatia!"

The princess tapped her fingers against the gold bands encircling her upper arms, lips pursed. Jagger knew the feeling—his sister could be exhausting.

"So, *Tatia*." Aria grinned at the girl. "Let's start over. I'm Aria Jones. This is my brother, Jagger. He woke up whack-a-doo in the middle of the night and, voila, here we are. So what's your story?"

Jagger rolled his eyes. He hated it when she acted older than him—or worse, smarter.

"Sister?" The girl's incredulous glance shifted back and forth from Jagger to Aria. "I see." Her posture—stiff and perfect—melted. Even her face seemed to relax. "I'm sorry, Aria Jones. I didn't summon you. I summoned your brother at the behest of the old gods. But the *Meseneh Rek* spell is powerful magic, and powerful magic can be ... fickle. I didn't intend to put you in danger. But in truth," she said, shaking her head. "Both of your lives were at risk whether I summoned you or not."

"What are you talking about?" Jagger leaned toward her.

"What do you mean our lives are at risk? And what Time Travel spell? You're telling me you can bend time? How?"

"Let's focus on the danger part." Aria poked him.

She had a point, but questions were swimming through his head like fish through the Chicago River. He wanted them answered. All of them. Now. "And what's this about 'the old gods?' Shouldn't you be loyal to your family's sun god, the Aten? I thought your dad banned all the old gods."

"That's true." The princess nodded, more casual now. "Pharaoh, my father, banned the traditional gods of Egypt. But I'm loyal to them still. They reward my loyalty. They've told me of the dangers we face. And they say you're the one who can save my family. I couldn't have cast the *Meseneh Rek* spell to start you on your quest without help from the same gods my father is working to banish, Jagger Jones."

And Jagger thought *he* had daddy issues!

"Whhhhhooooaaa. Wait!" Aria's eyes narrowed on the princess. She pulled a curl to her mouth—a dirty habit that usually meant she was thinking through a problem. "Tatia! I know you."

"Her name is Mer—"

"She can call me Tatia." The princess interrupted Jagger with a heavy sigh. "You can both call me whatever you like as long as you help me."

"We've met you before, haven't we?" Aria tugged her bottom lip.

"What?" Jagger shook his head. "How could we—"

"You're the mummy!" Aria said it like she'd just figured out the winning word in the spelling bee. "You're the mummy we saw in the tomb!"

KA-TASTROPHY

The princess stared down at her golden sandals, voice low. "I wish I were the mummy you saw. I would take her place if I could. But I can't undo what's been done to her. Come, you can meet her before ..." Whatever she was going to say, she decided against it. She slid primly onto the bed, pulling the white cover down to reveal the face of a younger girl, lips parted in deep sleep.

Jagger stifled a gasp. The girl looked almost exactly like Aria. *That's* what the princess had meant when she first saw Aria and mumbled that she looked like someone.

The Aria-look-alike-girl had a side ponytail like Tatia's. Amulets were scattered around her: a gold eye, a blue baboon, and a leafless tree made of red stone. This girl's face was sweeter than Tatia's somehow—fleshier, less stern.

"Oh, no." Aria fell to her knees by the bed, and leaned toward the sleeping girl.

"My younger sister, Meketaten. We call her Mek." Tatia's voice softened as she stared at her little sister.

Jagger's gut twisted.

"What's wrong with her?" Aria aimed her puppy-dog eyes at the younger princess. "Will she be okay?"

"Mek is dying. She'd be dead already it if were not for a magic elixir I've made with the help of the old gods. But she won't last much longer." Though the princess's voice quivered, she held her head high, eyes dry. "And that's not the worst part, Aria Jones. For us, life is a very short part of existence. We know the secrets of death, the path to the Heavenly Fields. Mek should enjoy a long afterlife where we'll be together again. But that too is being taken from her, a fate far worse than death." Her fierce stare shifted to Jagger. "And that's something we *can* solve. With your help, Jagger Jones, we can give Mek the afterlife she deserves."

"How?" Aria studied Mek like she was a stray animal Aria hoped to rescue. "What can Jagger do?"

"Do you know of the *Ka*?" Tatia asked.

Aria shook her head, turning to the princess with wide eyes.

"The body is made up of five parts: our Heart, our Shadow, our Name, our *Ba*, which houses our unique personalities, and our *Ka*, which is our unique essence, our living identity," the princess explained. "When we die, our *Ka* and *Ba* join, so we can travel to the Heavenly Fields. Without the joining, we can't enjoy an afterlife, a terrible fate for Egyptians. We spend our lives looking forward to sharing eternity with our loved ones."

"I'm not following this." Jagger shook his head. "Not the *Ka* part—that I know. And I'm really sorry about your sister. That sucks, really. But what does this have to do with us? And, uh, danger?"

The princess pulled the white sheet farther down, exposing an *ankh* amulet sitting on Mek's stomach. It was just like the one they'd seen in the tomb, but without the mysterious gemstones. "You touched this?"

"I did." Aria said before Jagger could respond.

The princess lifted a hand to her mouth, and nodded, like Aria had just offered a simple explanation of quadratic equations. "That explains how you got here."

"Did you bring us back through time with that cross-thingy?" Aria pointed at the *ankh*.

"It's an *ankh* amulet," Jagger corrected his sister before turning back to the princess. "And that can't possibly explain how we got here. I mean, what kind of scientific explanation …" He paused. "But I did hear your voice calling me. And your voice *was* coming from the amulet. But in our time it was covered in gemstones."

Tatia's eyes widened. "Gemstones," she muttered. She

shook herself, then nodded. "I cast the *Meseneh Rek* spell and summoned you, Jagger Jones. The old gods must have sent you a vision of the gemstones. That's useful." She stood up, pacing next to the bed. "I think I have an idea. Tell me about the gemstones you saw in your vision."

"Uh, okay." Jagger couldn't quite square visions sent by the gods with his steadfast belief in science. "I don't know. There were a bunch of them. And they sparkled. And there was a big, green one in the center."

"Were there nine of them?"

Jagger shook his head, mystified. "I don't remember."

"I bet there were nine." Tatia stopped pacing, and faced Jagger, who sunk onto the bed and watched the princess chew her lip, eyes narrowed in thought.

Jagger knew that nine—three threes—was a powerful number in ancient Egypt. That's why nine gods—an Ennead—sat atop the Egyptian pantheon. But what could that possibly have to do with …

"Gemstones make sense." The princess bobbed her head. "They have the perfect properties for such magic." She stared off to the side, like a movie was playing out of view. "Your vision means Mek's *Ka* is trapped inside the gemstones. My sister was poisoned by our enemy, the General, who ensnared her *Ka*."

"Who?" Jagger asked.

Tatia took a deep breath, then she spoke quickly, as if the

words would burn her tongue if she didn't get them out fast enough. "My father's trusted general. He wants to destroy our family and take Father's throne. The old gods have shown me the General's plan—he's going to use Mek's *Ka* to cast a spell that will annihilate our entire family. The *Heqa-oo Moot* is ugly magic, but powerful. We'll all die, but only Mek will be lost forever. The rest of us will meet again in the Heavenly Fields."

The Death Spell? The entire royal family of Amarna?

"Why?" Aria asked. "Why does this General guy want to kill your family?"

"The General longs for power." Tatia tossed a glance at her sister as she resumed pacing. "There's no power for a general in a time of peace, and Pharaoh's dedication to his sun god, the Aten, bars Egypt from engaging with foreign powers as our country traditionally has."

"Why doesn't your dad just fire him?" Jagger asked, twisting his head back and forth as he sat on the bed, watching Tatia march one way, pivot, then march the other way. "Or … whatever pharaohs do to generals who want to murder the royal family? Seems pretty reckless."

Tatia paused, and her eyes landed back on her sister. "My father won't hear a word against the General. Or anyone he believes serves the Aten faithfully. He doesn't believe me—"

"What about your mom, Queen Nefertiti?"

Tatia blinked quickly and shrugged narrow shoulders. "My parents won't listen to me. They think I'm a heretic. I think they're ignoring facts, because they don't want to face an uncomfortable truth."

Jagger squirmed. He knew that feeling. His dad had a bad habit of believing any crazy thing he could concoct to make himself look good while discounting, well, the truth—the truth usually made Dad look like a jerk. "That blows," Jagger mumbled.

"So what are you going to do?" Aria, perched on the end of Mek's bed, across from Jagger, snaked a hand out and touched the younger princess's bald head. Her other arm was wound around her giant, purple bag.

Tatia shifted her gaze to Aria, then to Jagger. "The General's spell will release a plague that will kill every member of the royal family, leaving the path to the throne open to him. Once we're all dead, he can wage war throughout the land. War is his heart's deepest desire. But the old gods say that you, Jagger Jones, can stop the spell. You must find the gemstones before the spell is cast and bring them back here before Mek transitions."

Find the gemstones? Stop some evil General's spell?

Why on Earth was any of this his job?

The request was so stunning it took Jagger a moment to find his voice. "Uh. Look, I'm really sorry about your sister. And your dad. All of it." He gulped. "My dad's also ..." He glanced at Aria—she shrugged. "Well, let's just say I get it. I mean, my sister is a pain in the butt, but I'd do anything to save her." He didn't look at Aria. He didn't need to. He knew she'd be wearing her cocky everyone-loves-me smile. "But I can't put her in danger. Mom would kill me. She's going to go through the roof when she wakes up, and realizes we're not there."

"Your sister is already in danger." The princess heaved a sigh. "The gods chose you, Jagger Jones, because you're royalty, a descendant of my family. If you're family, your sister is family."

"Wait! I'm a princess?" Aria clapped her hands, and her curls bounced as if they were just as excited. "Oh Tatia, we're family!" Aria beamed at the princess, looking her over as if auditioning her for the role of long-lost, big sis.

Jagger rolled his eyes. "How can that be?" he muttered, more to himself than the others, wondering which parent they'd inherited that connection from. Mom was the more likely candidate if only because her ancestors were from Africa. "But that means …" Jagger's heart plummeted. "No!"

"Yes." The princess nodded solemnly. "If the General's spell is successfully cast, every living member of the royal family will die. Every person from the bloodline who lived between this time and your own will be erased from history. None of us will survive."

Aria froze in place, the curl she was about to stick into her mouth fixed like a statue. "You mean if Jagger can't figure out how to stop this General and get the stones, we'll just disappear, like we were never born?" Her eyes flew to Jagger. "And you're sure *he's* the right guy? Is there gonna be math?"

"That's exactly right. None of us will survive if the General's spell is cast. The gods believe Jagger Jones is the only one who can deliver Mek and my family from the spell. *They* chose your brother, Aria Jones. Not me."

"Why me?" He mentally calculated the number of people in their shared family tree that would have lived between her time and his. "I mean, there has to be someone more, you know, hero-y than I am."

"I don't know why," she admitted. "But the gods have their reasons."

"But … but I don't even believe in your gods," he retorted.

She shrugged. "That doesn't make them any less real. Or less right."

The buzzing anxiety in Jagger's gut seeped into his head. It was like a cold-slurpy brain freeze speeding through his body. How was this happening?

"I'm asking a lot of you, Jagger Jones." The princess wove her fingers together in front of her face. "If I had another path, I'd take it. But the old gods say you're our only hope. They brought you to me. They gave you a vision. The gemstones you saw must be returned to Mek's amulet before she dies in order for her *Ka* and *Ba* to reunite. The magic elixir is losing its efficacy. It'll keep her alive for another week. No more. You must find the stones, and return them before Mek passes on."

He took a step back, away from her, as if she were a coiled cobra. "Let me get this straight." He folded his arms. "You want me, some guy from the future who knows nothing about your time except for what I've read in books, to find and return these *Ka*-infested gemstones before some evil General casts his Death Spell, and your sister dies? In one week? Is that all?"

She stared at him, chin high. "Before *our sisters* die."

He sagged. He wanted to do the right thing. But what *was* the right thing? Protecting Aria was right. That much was clear. But what was the best *way* to protect her? Being here was dangerous. What if her inhaler ran out, and she had an asthma attack in ancient Egypt? And what about Mom? Would she think he and Aria were dead in some Egyptian ditch? And Grams and Gramps? They were too old for this kind of drama. On the other hand, what if this girl was right? If he failed, there might be no Aria at all. What if he screwed up, and they all died?

Jagger's brain felt sluggish, but one idea stood out in stark relief, as big and bold as the Chicago skyline on a clear, summer day. "Send Aria back, and I'll help you."

"No way!" Aria exclaimed.

The princess dropped her gaze to the floor "I can't." Her voice cracked, and she cleared her throat. "The spell to return you to your time requires the gemstones. There's no way to send either of you back until we have them."

"So if we don't get them, we're stuck here?" Jagger asked

in disbelief. This was a trap! Why had she bothered to ask for his help if he had no choice?

"If we don't get them, we're DEAD! What part of this don't you get?" Aria was on the princess's side. Of course.

Jagger squirmed. He was caught. Even if his chances of successfully stopping some evil General from casting his spell, then getting the stones back before the younger princess died, were virtually nil, he had to try. He had to take care of his family. The princess might not count as family, but Mom and Aria did.

He rubbed the back of his neck. Then he nodded, feeling like someone had just tied his intestines in knots.

Aria flashed her you-made-the-right choice smile—the smile she wore whenever she got her way, which was ninety-two point seventy-eight percent of the time. How could she be happy about this?

"We're in." Aria beamed at her newfound cousin, one-billion-times-removed. "Now what?"

STRUCK BY AMULET-NING

"First, we must locate the gemstones." Tatia sounded like she was suggesting they go to the corner store for some bread. "The old gods sent Jagger a vision for a reason. If my hunch is correct, we might be able to use his vision to track the gemstones."

Jagger's throat felt tight. How was he going to find *Ka*-filled gemstones in a country that was foreign in every imaginable way, not to mention getting them away from some military expert with access to magic?

"Come." Tatia stood, and walked through an open door at the far end of the bedroom, waving for Jagger and Aria to follow. Jagger couldn't decide where to look as he trailed the princess through two smaller rooms that were empty of people but loaded with treasures. The walls were painted with trees and animals, like the outside world had wormed its way inside.

"This is where you live?" Aria asked breathlessly.

"Yes. We're in my quarters at the palace," Tatia clarified, leading them into a cozy study with a cedar desk and four low chairs, each covered with soft leather, grouped around a gold table. The smell of cedar tickled Jagger's nose. The princess rummaged through an alabaster chest that sat on the desk, pulling out a small, red, stone amulet shaped like an *ankh* but with a knot in the center. "This should help us find the gemstones, Jagger Jones."

"The Knot of Isis." Jagger recognized the symbol.

"I've heard of Isis. She's a goddess!" Aria said as she sunk onto a chair.

"Yeah, lil' sis." Jagger was grudgingly impressed Aria remembered who Isis was. "She was a trickster. Her evil brother, Seth, chopped her husband up and scattered his body parts. Isis tracked down every bit of him and put him back together so they could have a son. Their son is the falcon god, Horus."

"Good. You know of our history." Tatia held the Knot of Isis out to Jagger. "Isis is the wisest of the old gods. This is one of my family's most prized possessions, given to me by my grandmother."

"Grand … grandmother?" he sputtered. "You mean

Queen Tiye?" Jagger cringed at the naked enthusiasm in his voice. But come on, Queen Tiye was one of the most fascinating historical figures of all time.

Tatia nodded. "Grandmother still worships the old gods, as I do. She trained me in magic, despite my parents' disapproval. She also taught me not to be fooled by appearances. This is one of Egypt's most magical objects."

Jagger reached out, entranced by the plain amulet, spinning from a leather ribbon.

When his hand closed around it, Tatia shut her eyes and began chanting, "Come, Isis. Come, Heka …"

Jagger didn't know if he should sit next to his sister or remain standing, facing the princess. He shifted on his feet, clutching the amulet and feeling awkward. As if she read his thoughts, Tatia put a hand on his shoulder. Then she released him, and pulled out a larger gold amulet hanging from a chain around her neck. Shaped like an eye, it had an arched brow, a short vertical line emerging from the bottom, and a longer curly loop shooting off to the side. A blue gem sat where the pupil should be.

"I remember seeing an eye-thing like that in the museum," Aria said.

"Ssshhhh." Jagger hushed her. How could he figure out what Tatia was up to when Aria wouldn't shut up? "It's the Eye of Horus."

Chanting louder, as if she also wanted to drown Aria

out, Tatia circled her hand over the eye amulet. "See us, Isis. Come, Horus. Join us, Heka. Judge this boy worthy of your magic."

Colorful lights erupted overhead, sparkling above Jagger's head, drifting up toward the blue and gold ceiling. The lights reminded Jagger of the ones that had danced inside the gemstones: purple, blue, yellow, red, green, pink, orange. The smell of mint and eucalyptus filled the air, overpowering the scent of cedar.

"Cool," Aria breathed. She let her head fall back against the high-backed chair, staring up.

Jagger squeezed the Isis Knot amulet tighter in his sweaty palm, feeling nervous. Was this safe?

The princess aimed the Horus Eye at Jagger.

And then things got weird.

The blue gem faded to brown. The gold melted and was replaced by flesh. It looked like a real eye with a black pupil.

Jagger wasn't imagining this. The thing was *looking* at them.

"It blinked!" Aria cried.

She was right. The eye really had blinked. Jagger shifted closer to his sister.

"The gods see you, Jagger Jones. Let's hope I'm right and they want you to have the Isis Knot. If Isis and Heka transfer the amulet's power to you, you may be able to locate the gemstones from your vision."

The princess opened her arms wide, still clutching the Horus Eye. The room was so small, Tatia's outstretched arms filled nearly half the space, her fingers extending over Aria's head.

Aria squealed as a bright ball of white light emerged from Tatia's chest and hovered over her. Aria sat up taller, reaching out a finger as if she wanted to pop it.

"Stop!" Jagger hunched his shoulders, staring at the giant, floating light with his mouth hanging open. He took another step back, putting himself between the light and Aria.

"It's pretty." Aria clapped her hands. "Can I touch it?"

"No!" Jagger shot back as the ball of light shifted directions and floated toward him like an enormous, bloated firefly out for blood. "It's not safe," he mumbled. It was the size of Aria's old, stuffed frog and bright enough to make Jagger wish he was wearing sunglasses.

"It *is* safe, Jagger Jones," Tatia corrected him. "It's a *Seshep ny Netjer*—"

"God's Light?" Jagger heard the proper noun in Egyptian, like the spell names. Titles, he figured. Learning a new language via magic was a trip.

She nodded. "All magic is animated by a *Seshep ny Netjer*. That is true for magical things and magical people, although very few things or people have one. The amulet is bonded to me through its *Seshep ny Netjer*. But it's considering you now." Jagger thought he detected a hint of concern in her voice.

"You must let it in, Jagger Jones. Open yourself to the gods."

Jagger took another step back, butting up against the table. He didn't want that light touching him. Besides, even if he wanted to, he had no idea how to "open himself to the gods."

The light seemed unsure as well. Just as it neared Jagger, it slowed, as if considering his worthiness.

Tatia scowled. Maybe it wouldn't work after all. Maybe they could forget this whole thing, and he could take Aria home.

Faster than a strike of lightning, the light split in two.

Jagger sucked in a breath.

Tatia shook her head. "What …"

Two smaller balls of light lingered above him, bouncing gently. They paused, in tandem, then rushed into Jagger's chest.

He gasped and clawed at his chest. Even though he didn't feel the lights enter him, it still freaked him out. "What is it?" He wanted that thing out of him. Now!

"I don't …" The princess was staring at him like *he* was the museum curiosity.

A tugging sensation struck him. He stilled his hands, took a deep breath, and focused on his body. It was as if an invisible string connected him to the Knot of Isis amulet held in his left hand. He lifted his hand and stared at it, dumbfounded. What was happening? Jagger had no idea if this God's Light was good or evil. Was it sentient? How?

"Did it work?" Aria asked. He could hear the envy in

her voice, as if being infested by some ancient ball of light was another experience she didn't want to miss, like tracking rhinos in Namibia—one of Aria's favorite Jones family adventures.

He looked to the princess for an answer, even though it was pretty clear something had just happened.

Tatia cocked her head to the side. "I've never seen a *Seshep ny Netjer* split." She shook her head. "But even I have only encountered them a few times. They stick to the person or thing they're bonded too. It's odd though." She narrowed her eyes on Jagger. "I suppose the gods' mysteries are endless."

"But did it work?" Aria repeated.

"That part worked." Tatia nodded.

Jagger couldn't take his eyes off the Isis Knot amulet in his hand. How was he *feeling* the connection? His mind searched for anything scientific that could explain it.

"Now *you* hold the Isis Knot's power, Jagger Jones," the princess continued. "The magic will only work for you, and it will only help you locate people and things you've experienced. Let's hope your vision of the gemstones is sufficient to let you track them."

"So cool," Aria breathed. "Can I get one?"

Tatia slid down on the chair next to her, but she didn't reward Aria's ridiculous request with a response. "Hold the amulet. Calm and focus your mind. Picture the gemstones we need to find."

Jagger felt like scarabs were running up his arm, but he did as he was told—grasping the Isis Knot and trying to focus his mind. It was a little hard to think about jewelry when you were stuck three thousand years in the past with your too-vulnerable little sister and some mysterious God's Light infesting your body.

Nothing happened.

He squeezed his eyes shut. As insane as it seemed, he had to try. If Tatia was right, that jewelry could wipe out his entire family. He needed to do everything he could to help them. He heard Mom in his head: *Breathe*. He inhaled through his nose, letting it slowly out through his mouth. He tried to put Aria out of his mind by visualizing the gemstones' ghostlike appearance and sparkling lights.

An image of the large malachite swam before his eyes.

"Whoa!" A pulling sensation hit him. "That way." Jagger pointed. He opened his eyes, struggling to orient himself in the small, unfamiliar room. Was that south?

Tatia grinned. She jumped up and grabbed a map of Egypt off the desk, spreading it out on the gold table. "Good," she said. "Now keep the gemstones in your mind, and show me where they are on this map."

The feeling shifted, triangulating. Jagger leaned over his sister, letting his finger roam over the map. He could *feel* their location. For a moment, he lost his sense of direction. Grasping the amulet tighter, he returned his thoughts to the gemstones and let his finger slide southward, landing on a familiar city.

"Thebes." A smile lit the princess's face. "That's excellent news. Herihor can help."

"Herihor?" Jagger shook his hand as the sensation faded. The smell of mint and eucalyptus was gone too. He glanced up; the colorful lights had also vanished.

"That was magic!" Aria's eyes were wide. "Is magic always pretty? Does it always smell yummy?"

Jagger ignored her. Her questions were legit, but he had a more important one. "Who's Herihor?"

"The High Priest of the old god, Amun-Ra, at Thebes," the princess explained, perching on a cedar chair and resting her arms on the gold table. "He's a powerful man and a trusted ally. Like me, Herihor longs for the return of the old gods. He's kept Amun-Ra's priesthood strong in Thebes, where Pharaoh has not yet managed to stamp out the old gods' power. I'll send a letter of introduction." She reached over to the desk and mined a papyrus scroll and a scribal kit from a small chest. After dipping her reed pen in the jar of black ink, she scrawled on the scroll. "Herihor is nearly impossible to get to. But he won't refuse my wishes."

"Can he do magic too?" Aria's eyes were bright. "Can you teach me? Can we do more?"

Jagger shook his head. He didn't like it. Everything about this situation was too inexplicable, too unfamiliar, too unscientific. How could he feel the presence of some gemstones hundreds of miles away?

Plus, he knew what was coming next. "We're going to Thebes, aren't we?"

"No, Jagger Jones." Tatia looked up from the scroll. "*You* are going to Thebes."

"Wait, what?" Jagger's heart thumped. "You're sending me to Thebes alone? You're not coming?"

She shook her head. "If your association with me is revealed, the two of you will be in even more danger. Anything of interest to me will attract the General like a beetle to dung."

"But—"

"Well *I'm* going too!" Aria sat up straighter, pounding her fists on the table.

"Yes, Aria Jones. You're going." Tatia's eyes twinkled. "And so is the Protector."

DRESSED TO … KIDNAP?

"The Protector?" Aria leaned toward Tatia eagerly. "The Protector is magical too, right?"

"Yes." The princess nodded. "One of our most accomplished magicians."

"Can everyone here do magic?" Aria's eyes sparkled.

The princess shook her head. "No. The gift is mostly limited to my family. I'm the most gifted magician our family has produced in generations. But there are a few others, outside of the family, who have the gift, although only the strongest magicians have power now. Father has successfully installed his new god, the Aten, throughout the country. The power of the old gods fades as the Aten's rises." She released a heavy sigh. "The General is evil, but he has no magic.

Someone must be working with him, a magician powerful enough to cast the *Heqa-oo Moot*."

Great. Jagger dropped his head in his hands. "Okay. So who's helping him? Is it someone from your family?"

"I don't know. As I say, magicians are rare, especially now, but the gods weren't compelled to tell me who is working with the General." She rolled the scroll and tapped it against the gold table, lips tight.

"Were the gods compelled to share *anything* useful?" Jagger's voice cracked.

One side of Tatia's lips curved up. "They shared you."

Aria smiled approvingly. "When do we meet this Protector?"

Tatia glanced at the open door that led back out to her bedroom. "Soon." She shifted her attention back to Jagger, examining him like a bug under a microscope. He glanced down at his dirty jeans and T-shirt, squirming self-consciously. "You'll stand out like trees in a desert like that. Come."

She stood and led them back to a small room sandwiched between the study, where they'd just been, and her bedroom, where Mek was still lying. Aria stood next to him, bouncing on the balls of her feet, as Tatia opened a tall wardrobe that was painted with images of the goddess Hathor depicted as a cow-headed woman. It had gold knobs and small, ivory square inlays. Tatia hunted through it and pulled out piles of linens and diaphanous materials and leather sandals.

"Are we getting makeovers?" Aria squealed happily, hugging her purse to her chest.

Jagger moaned as Tatia draped a dress over his sister. The answer was obvious.

Aria was thrilled with the white gown and elaborate jewels the princess gave her, even happier when she got made up to look like an ancient Egyptian princess. Things got iffy when Tatia wanted to shave Aria's head. Aria didn't care if kids in Egypt were bald. She was dedicated to her thick curls. After a short but frightening stare-down, Tatia caved to Aria's will, just as Mom had every time she and Aria disagreed on her clothing. The princess braided Aria's hair into cornrows and placed a blue and gold headband on her head. His sister looked like a pint-sized Cleopatra.

"No." Jagger shook his head when Tatia turned to him and lifted a blade to his hair. "I've been growing my 'fro. You're not touching it."

"You'll draw unwanted attention with that hair," the princess insisted.

"I'm used to that." He backed away from the princess and her blade. "We know how to blend in. We're from Chicago." He paused. "It's, you know, diverse."

Tatia cocked her head to the side.

"We're biracial," he explained. "Our mom is black, and our dad is white."

The princess shrugged. "Your hair is fine, Jagger Jones.

But it's not long enough to braid. We must cut it."

"I don't want to cut it." He put his hands on his head. The last time someone had suggested Jagger cut his hair, he was sitting on a stage with five other kids, staring out at an audience. A guy from the opposing debate team had used Jagger's hair in his argument, comparing the government's need to trim its "out of control" budget with Jagger's supposed need for a haircut. Jagger never forgot how it felt to be singled out for something that was a part of him in front of all those people. Kids snickered, judges wiggled in discomfort, and Grams sagged with sadness. Mom looked like she wanted to go all mama bear on the kid. But it was Gramps' reaction that steeled Jagger's spine. Gramps smiled. And that smile gave Jagger exactly what he needed in that moment. His hair might not have looked like that of the other debaters, but it didn't make him any less smart, or less responsible, or less competent. Gramps' smile was a way of reminding Jagger of something Gramps often said to him: *always remember you're descended from kings and queens, so hold your head high and act like the royalty you are.* At the time, Jagger couldn't have imagined how right Gramps was. But that smile was enough. When it was Jagger's turn to respond, he flipped the kid's argument on its head. A few hours later, Jagger walked out of that debate tournament with a humbled opponent, a first place trophy, and newfound pride in his 'fro.

But the princess didn't care about his sentimental

attachment to his hair. Her chin jutted out. "Do you want to save our sisters?"

"But ..." He shuffled his feet. "Can't I save our sisters *and* keep my hair?"

Tatia folded her arms, glaring at him through tightened eyes. "Do you think you'll get through the task ahead without sacrifice?" Her voice was stern. "Surely your hair doesn't mean more to you than my sister? More than your sister?" She stared down at her feet, blinking quickly, before glancing back up at him and lifting the blade higher.

Jagger sagged. She was right. He blew out a puff of air and nodded.

Minutes later, he was left with stubble. His head felt too light. And *then* came the makeup! He knew boys in ancient Egypt wore makeup, but he hadn't given it much thought until Tatia insisted on lining his eyes with kohl.

When she was done with him, Aria couldn't stop laughing. He was irritated, but who could blame her? He looked ridiculous in a dress, with more makeup than hair.

The hazing would've lasted longer but for a knock on the bedroom door. Tatia left them in the adjacent room, warning them to stay silent as she rushed to open the door. She returned a moment later with a large woman waddling along behind her.

Jagger froze, examining the newcomer. She had a wide, flat nose. Sweat ran down the folds of her three chins—her neck fat swung back and forth as she strode forward. She moved fast for such a big woman. She wore a white, tent-sized muumuu and a black wig cut into a short bob with blunt bangs. Golden chains dripped from her fleshy neck and arms.

"She's the Protector?" Aria's eyes were wide.

"No." Tatia shook her head. "This is my dear friend and loyal ally, Wenher."

"When-Hair?" Aria whispered to Jagger as Tatia added a long string of titles loaded with phrases like *beloved of the Aten* and *esteemed by the Great Royal Mother*. "Aren't there any Caseys or Mias or Zoes around here?"

Jagger rolled his eyes, watching the woman as she shifted her glance from him to his sister.

"I was expecting only one." The woman sounded like she'd spent her life smoking cigarettes in one of Chicago's grungiest blues clubs.

"Yes," Tatia said dryly. "So was I."

Wenher grunted. "No matter. I'll get them where they need to go without attracting attention. That's more than you could do." One side of her fleshy lips quirked up.

Tatia thanked her, then pivoted, placing her hands on Jagger's shoulders. "You have one week, Jagger Jones. You must return to me then. With the gemstones."

Jagger felt faint as he did the math. An Egyptian week was ten days long. It was about four hundred kilometers from Amarna to Thebes. At best, a good boat could cover seventy kilometers a day, which meant five days of sailing to get there. Coming back would be faster: the wind on the Nile blew north, toward Amarna. Still, that was brutal math, even for him. On the bright side, they'd only have to deal with returning in time if they managed to get the stones, which must be one of history's longest long shots.

"But ... what ..." Jagger couldn't find the words. He was still trying to wrap his head around his family's pending doom, and now the girl who'd dragged him into this was sending them across the country alone.

"Wenher will take you to the Protector," the princess promised. "The Protector will get you to Thebes. Once there, Herihor will help you." She handed Jagger the scroll. "Don't lose this. This letter of introduction will get you into the temple. Once in Thebes, you can use the amulet to pinpoint precisely where the gemstones are."

Jagger ran his hand over his stubbly head, trying to unglue his tongue from the roof of his mouth.

"Will we see you again?" Aria's puppy-dog expression was back.

"You will, Aria Jones. You'll return with the gemstones. We'll save my sister."

"And then you'll send us home," Jagger added.

Tatia turned away, waving at Wenher, who rushed them out through the bedroom, where Jagger snuck a peek at the slumbering Mek, then through the bedroom door, past several stern looking guards, and down maze-like halls, painted in colorful images of the royal family. Jagger made an effort to shut his mouth. He should act normal, but they were inside the royal palace of Amarna! The big woman hustled them out a massive entrance and onto a horse-drawn carriage, just big enough for Jagger and Aria to stand next to her.

Jagger jumped onto the carriage next to Wenher, who reeked of sweat and honey. He turned back at the sound of children. Several kids spilled out from the enormous, gold palace doors. Two young girls giggled madly as a slightly older pair—a girl and a boy with a limp—chased them, the stern guards shifting to let the kids weave between them. The smallest girl stopped to pet Wenher's horse. She reminded Jagger of a younger Aria. He smiled as she flashed an adorable grin at the big woman.

"I must go now, dear ones," Wenher said, swiveling her neck to stare at one girl, then the next. "I'll visit you and your mother, the Queen, soon. Perhaps we can convince her to let you two come riding with me."

The two smallest girls clapped their hands with delight as the largest girl nodded her thanks.

"Meretaten's other sisters, the three youngest princesses, and their half-brother, Prince Tutankamun," the woman explained as she grabbed the reins of the two black horses and led them out the large gate, through a line of palace guards.

Jagger craned his neck to look back at the boy king, famous

for his tomb, the only intact royal tomb ever discovered, and his sisters. Then he remembered some evil General was out there, hoping to murder these adorable little kids—and it was Jagger's job to stop him—and his stomach plummeted into his toes.

"*The* King Tut?" Aria whispered to Jagger.

Jagger nodded as Wenher led the chariot out of the palace gate and onto a wide street. He stared, mouth ajar, back at the palace, built of white stone and covered in brightly painted reliefs of the royal family. A painted stone gate circled the perimeter, and dozens of statues of Pharaoh Akhenaten stretched the length of the wall.

People streamed around them on the street. There were men with white kilts and bare chests. Women in simple, ankle-length dresses held up by a few straps passed them by. A dour old man mumbled to himself, a harried looking young woman hushed two small children, and three young boys with their bald heads together laughed while a black dog bounced at their feet.

Jagger tried to take it all in as he clung tightly to the chariot's rail. He felt a little foolish when he noticed Aria holding her hands above the rail, balancing like she was on a rollercoaster.

They'd only gone a few blocks when Wenher's gasp pulled him out of his trance. She flicked the reins, prompting the horses to move faster. Sweat dappled her forehead, and she cursed under her breath.

"What's wrong?" Aria grabbed the chariot's rail.

"The General's soldiers," Wenher whispered under her breath, as if the two soldiers, blocking the road in front of them where the main street intersected a smaller cross street, might hear her.

The men wore gray kilts with leather thongs crossing their chests. Both held a staff at his side. One was brawny and the other one, holding up a hand, was scrawny and bald. There wasn't another chariot in sight.

The soldiers were stopping them.

"We can't pass," Wenher moaned through clenched teeth as she slowed the horses. "What is the meaning of this?" Her voice rang out regally.

"Excuse us, my lady," the scrawny soldier said, eyeing Jagger and Aria. "The General has had a report of suspicious activity involving two kids from out of town."

Wenher's shoulders drew back. "Are you accusing my niece and nephew of something, sir? They are *nobles*! Visiting from Memphis. We've just come from the palace. Perhaps you would like to take this to the family?" she drawled.

Jagger moaned. Was he really being profiled in ancient Egypt? It wasn't the first time—he'd been stopped twice just for walking through Andrew's hoity-toity neighborhood— but come on! Jagger held his breath, hoping the soldier would be intimidated by the name-dropping and let them pass.

"That won't be necessary," Scrawny replied with a smirk.

His silky voice didn't match his scruffy appearance. "We'll just ask them a few questions to confirm they're not the kids we're looking for."

Jagger's gut churned as Scrawny eyeballed him. Aria leaned against him. Wenher cleared her throat and glanced at Jagger.

He nodded, patting the scroll tucked into his kilt. What choice did he have?

"Make it quick." Wenher fanned herself with a stubby, bejeweled hand.

Jagger licked his dry lips, wondering how a rich, well-connected teenager from ancient Memphis would behave. He copied Wenher's posture and mimicked that cocky kid from math camp he didn't like.

Before Scrawny could utter a word, Aria shouldered Jagger aside. "What do you want?" she said.

Jagger stifled a moan. He didn't know if he was impressed with the steel in her voice or hurt that she assumed he couldn't handle this. Scrawny's sneer made him feel even more emasculated. *Perfect.*

"Where are you from, little girl?"

"My aunt just told you," Aria shot back. "We're from Memphis, here to visit the royal family and devote ourselves to the …" Aria stumbled, trying to remember the name of a god whose name she'd first heard of a few hours ago.

"The Aten," Jagger finished.

"What part of Memphis?"

Aria reached for a curl but they were all tucked neatly into her braids. She fake-coughed as Jagger searched his memory. The only thing he knew about ancient Memphis was that it had, from time to time, been the country's capital and was located near the famous pyramids. He couldn't have mentioned a section of the city had his life depended on it, which, he realized, it might.

"Different parts," he squeaked. He cleared his throat. "Our father owns several villas. One has a view of Khufu's pyramid. Perhaps you want to involve him?" Jagger tried doubling down on Wenher's threats.

The soldier chuckled. Apparently he wasn't scared of their imaginary daddy. "And where were you last night, around sundown?"

Jagger had been in the modern world playing on his phone and ignoring his chores, because he was mad at Mom. But that wasn't the answer this guy was looking for.

"The Great Royal Mother has generously arranged this visit for my niece and nephew," Wenher interrupted before Jagger could make an even bigger fool of himself. "As you must know, my husband, the great Huya, Overseer of the quarters of the Great Queen, Favorite of the Lord of the Two Lands ..." Jagger wondered what social rules were at work here as the long string of titles spewed from Wenher's mouth. How many titles could one man have?

"That's enough." The soldier banged his staff on the ground. "The General is going to want to talk to these two." He waved his buddy, Brawny, forward.

"I will not hand over my charges." Wenher lifted her head high as Brawny approached.

"I assure you, my lady." Scrawny's smile was sly. "They'll be safe with us. We're taking them to the General. Surely you trust the General with your niece and nephew? You know of his devotion to the Aten—a devotion he shares with Pharaoh. We wouldn't want to tell Pharaoh you stood in the way of the Aten's desires."

Jagger's heart was banging against his chest. Aria grabbed his hand—her hand was sweaty.

Wenher flinched. "Of course I trust the General—" she stuttered.

"Then there's no problem," the soldier interrupted. "We'll return them to you. Right after the General clears them. I'm sure everything you've said here is true, so it won't take long."

Wenher looked over at Jagger with a clenched jaw and an apologetic expression.

Brawny lifted a hand to help Aria down.

Jagger was frozen. They couldn't go with these guys, but they couldn't say no without looking guilty.

"Now, little girl." Scrawny's voice was hard.

Jagger sagged as his sister folded her arms, and stepped down from the chariot.

7

FOLLOW YOUR PRINCE-IBLES

Brawny's fingers dug into Jagger's arm. Jagger was so focused on Aria—stomping along in Scrawny's clutches in front of him—he barely noticed.

"Are you from Amarna?" Aria flashed the soldier her most winning you-gotta-love-me smile, and Jagger's heart dropped. No one that guy's age was *from* Amarna. It was built from scratch on untouched land. Jagger wasn't sure how many years ago that was, but it was fewer years than this guy had been alive.

"Sure." Scrawny's mouth curved into a grin. "Born and raised here—"

"How far away is the General?" Jagger's voice cracked as he interrupted the soldier's lie before his sister could dig her grave deeper.

Scrawny peeked back at him and snickered.

"No questions," Brawny responded in a surprisingly kind tone. He glanced over at Jagger and loosened his grip.

"You guys asked questions," Jagger retorted. He needed to buy time. And he needed to get his sister away from that creep *before* he threw her in front of an evil General dedicated to murdering their family.

"We're in charge." Brawny's voice was high for such a beefy guy.

"I thought the royal family was in charge." Jagger scanned the terrain. Houses with red doors lined the street. A few had clay snakes protecting them. Fewer people were around but those who were tossed glances their way as the soldiers dragged them past. Jagger called up a map of ancient Amarna in his head. The wide boulevard that ran between the main palace and the small Aten temple was behind them. The Nile was to the west. So they must be in the residential neighborhood just south of the main city.

"We work for the General," Brawny explained. "And the General works for Pharaoh."

"So that means we're in charge," Scrawny finished. "Back to your sister's question—"

"No it doesn't!" Jagger was too loud. "It doesn't mean you're in charge. I mean, technically. It means you do the bidding of the General, who does the bidding of the Pharaoh. So you're not in charge—"

"We're in charge of you." Scrawny yanked Aria closer, and Jagger's heart sped up.

"We …" Brawny stopped suddenly. His fingers tightened on Jagger's arm.

A chariot sped toward them.

"The prince!" Brawny hissed as he pulled Jagger to the side of the street and dropped to his knees. He yanked Jagger's arm, forcing him down as Scrawny followed, dragging a squirming Aria. Brawny cast his eyes down, but Scrawny stared at the gold chariot hurtling their way, pulled by a white horse.

Aria fell to her knees beside Jagger. He leaned into her, heart thumping. He could feel her bag, which she'd slid under her white shift dress.

His mind raced. *In the midst of chaos, there is also opportunity.* The words of the famous Chinese general, Sun Tzu, thundered through his head.

This was his chance.

The chariot rumbled closer.

Just as it reached them, Jagger pulled away from the soldier and raced toward the horse.

Dust flew.

The horse neighed.

His sister screamed.

Green lights erupted to Jagger's right side, and the horse reared back. Its hooves were so close to his head, Jagger felt the wind of the horse's sudden lurch.

"Whoa!" The voice was young but gravely.

Jagger opened one eye. He was in the middle of the road, hunched up and frozen. But he was alive. He hadn't been trampled by a horse.

"What are you doing?" A stern faced teenager jumped off the chariot. He looked like he was a few years older than Jagger and was covered in gold, from head to toe. Even his sandals were gold. He stared at Jagger through kohl-lined eyes over crossed arms. "What …"

Jagger sucked in a breath. He peeked over at Aria and realized even Scrawny had his head down now. Only Aria was looking up, hand to her mouth. When their eyes met, she jumped up, pulled away from the soldier, and ran to Jagger.

"My sister," Jagger stuttered. "I mean … I'm sorry." He dropped to the ground, mimicking the soldiers. He felt Aria kneel next to him and slipped an arm around her.

"What is the meaning of this?" the boy asked.

"I'm sorry, your, uh, sir." Jagger had no idea how to address an ancient Egyptian prince. "I … uh …"

"You're Tatia's … I mean, Meretaten's brother?" Aria was staring up at the prince, head quirked to one side. At least she hadn't called the princess Merry Hot One this time.

Jagger braved a glance at the boy. His eyebrows were crawling up his face. His nostrils flared as he examined Aria, then shifted his focus to Jagger.

"And King Tut's brother," she added.

Jagger shoved his shoulder into her. How slow could she be? Even Aria should be able to figure out this kid was older than Tut. So for Tut to be king, this kid had to be dead.

"Smenkare!" Jagger shouted the name as it came to him. There wasn't much scholarship about Tut's older brother, who'd died young. "We know who you are, Prince Smenkare. Please ignore my sister. She's delusional." He squeezed Aria's shoulder, willing her to shut up.

"What …" The prince shook his head in confusion and glanced at the soldiers, now crowded behind Jagger and Aria.

"We're sorry, sir." Scrawny was suddenly respectful. "We're taking them to the General. He wants to talk to them."

"The General?" Smenkare squinted.

"Yes, sir." Scrawny kept his eyes down as he nodded.

"You're telling me the General wants these two kids?" The prince twined his fingers together, eyes glowing.

"Yes, sir." Scrawny nodded.

"Well." The prince studied Jagger through hooded eyes. "Then the General shall have them."

Jagger's heart dropped. Maybe General Sun Tzu wasn't as brilliant as his reputation.

"Thank you, sir." Scrawny put his hands on Aria, and she twisted. "We're sorry they bothered you."

"No bother," Smenkare drawled. "Put them on my chariot."

"What?" Scrawny's head wobbled. "Sir, the General is waiting—"

"I understand." Smenkare hissed. "I said, put these two on my chariot. Now!"

The soldiers shifted back and forth, exchanging confused glances. Scrawny shook his head.

"Yes, sir." Brawny pulled Jagger up, and led him to the horse that had almost trampled him.

Aria scrambled up onto the chariot, and Jagger jumped in behind her.

"Did you see that green light? That was magic!" Aria whispered. "He's the Protector."

"We don't know that," Jagger shot back, patting his thigh to confirm the scroll hadn't fallen out during his brush with death. "He just said he's taking us to the General. We can't trust this kid."

"Then why did you do it?"

"Because those soldiers were *definitely* taking us the wrong way. Our odds were better—"

"Seriously?" She sighed. "What, did you do math in your head and decide tossing yourself in front of a running horse was a winning plan? If fancy-teenager-boy hadn't done, well, whatever that green light was, that horse would have killed you."

"Just stay quiet, and let me do the talking," he shot back as Smenkare climbed into the chariot.

The prince urged the horses on without sparing Jagger or Aria a glance.

Jagger gripped the rail behind him, keeping his distance from the prince. He stared back at the soldiers as they sped off. The urge to flash Scrawny a rude gesture was hard to resist. At least they were headed toward the palace. If they could just get to Tatia, or Wenher, before the General …

"You know my sister?" Smenkare kept his eyes straight ahead.

"We—"

Jagger stomped on Aria's toe before she could say something stupid. His mind raced.

The prince glanced back at them, impatient.

"Uh," Jagger stuttered. "The palace is lovely. Are we going there?" His chest felt too tight.

The prince's smile was inscrutable, but Jagger felt a little better when he caught a glimpse of the palace ahead. Before they reached it, the prince turned toward the Nile, leading the horse to two large docks that jetted out into the river. Several impressive looking sailboats with huge, white sails stood out among numerous smaller fishing boats. Men crawled all over the big ships like ants on a hill, loading and unloading goods.

Smenkare stopped the horse and pointed to the largest boat.

Jagger looked back at the palace.

"Come with me." The prince jumped down and nodded at the ship as a nearby soldier took his horse's reins.

The ship had two wooden structures, like small barns,

one on the front and the other on the back. Small windows ran along the top of the boat's deck, each with an oar sticking straight through it.

Jagger stumbled off the chariot, his sister at his side. "Where are we going?" His heart raced as he glanced from Smenkare to the boat.

"Thebes." Smenkare smiled.

The Protector?

"You're—"

"Aria!" Jagger turned on his sister. "Remember, lil' sis, that you're sick. I'm here to take care of you. Let. Me. Speak."

She scowled. But at least she shut up.

"Come." Smenkare motioned them forward, then pivoted and strode across a thin plank onto the ship's deck.

Jagger paused. What should he do? Could Smenkare be the Protector Tatia told them about? If so, why didn't the prince just say that? Still, he wasn't taking them to the General. Or was he? This wasn't the way the soldiers had been heading. And what were the chances the prince would rush them to a boat bound for Thebes if he wasn't the Protector?

Jagger fingered the letter to Herihor. If he got to Thebes, he could find the temple and get the High Priest's help. Of course, they'd also be further away from home, further away from Mom.

"He's the Protector," Aria murmured. "He's going to Thebes. And he knows magic. And he's her brother!"

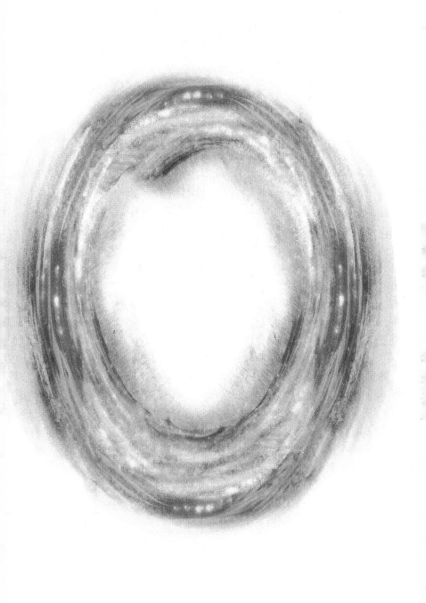

"I don't know." Jagger sighed, glancing from the ship back to the palace.

Aria put her hands on her hips and glared at him. "Mek has one week, Jagger. We don't have time for analysis paralysis. You need to trust people—"

"Yeah, because that's worked out so well for me so far."

"This isn't about Dad," she moaned, glancing at Smenkare, who was on the ship's deck, staring back at them. With a huff, she stuck out her chin. "I don't care what you do. I'm going."

She turned and ran gracefully over the plank, toward a very pleased looking prince.

DON'T HATE ME 'CAUSE I'M MUT-IFUL

A man with dimples, happy eyes, and a lithe, muscular body strolled up just as Jagger jumped onto the ship's deck next to his sister. The man's black hair was speckled with silver, and the lines around his eyes suggested both age and sun. Late thirties, Jagger guessed.

"These two will be joining me." Smenkare's eyes moved past the man to scan the shore as he motioned toward Jagger and Aria.

"I'm Babi, the captain." The man nodded. He had a wide smile and perfect, white teeth.

"At least I can pronounce it," Aria mumbled to Jagger before plastering an I'm-adorable look on her face and turning to the captain. "I'm Aria Jones. And this is my brother, Jagger."

Babi's eyebrows drew together. "Unusual names." He glanced at Smenkare.

"Yes. Yes, they are." The prince's eyes crept up Jagger then slid down Aria. The look made Jagger's skin crawl. "Now." Smenkare's gravelly voice was authoritative. "I'm in a bit of a rush, Captain. If you don't mind casting off?"

The captain's smile stiffened. "Of course." He glanced toward the bustling harbor. "We'll set sail shortly."

"We'll set sail now!" The prince may, or may not, be the Protector, but he clearly thought he was the boss.

Babi's smile looked forced. "As you wish, my prince." He barked commands at sailors, ordering them to prepare the ship to sail.

"So, Smell-ka ..." Aria paused, obviously stumped by the prince's name.

"She means ..." Jagger squirmed, wracking his brain for words that would interrupt his sister and not sound idiotic. "We're wondering ... where the General is. And where we'll stay." Jagger looked around. What if the General was on this ship? "Why are you going to Thebes?"

"Quickly, Captain," the prince ordered, ignoring Jagger's stream of questions before turning back to Aria. "Tell me all about yourself, child. How do you know my sister?"

"She brought us here. Are you—"

"Aria!" Jagger grabbed her arm. "Don't be rude. The prince asked about you. You gotta tell him the truth. You know, about your dementia. And how you like to make up creative stories."

She rolled her eyes as the ship shifted, slowly disconnecting from the dock.

"Sorry about my sister." Jagger's brain was whirling. "But hey, I don't have to tell you about sisters, right?"

The prince grunted.

"You know how they are. You and your oldest sister, what kind of relationship—"

"WAIT!"

Jagger spun toward the voice—it sounded like tinkling bells and summertime.

The most beautiful woman he'd ever seen landed gracefully on the ship's deck. She'd made the six-foot jump from the dock as easily as if she were stepping off a curb on Chicago's Michigan Avenue after a million-dollar shopping spree.

And that wasn't even the weird part.

Two men leapt after her. A huge gust of wind—it smelled like fresh flowers—carried them forward. They rolled onto the deck, then jumped up, and stood flanking her. They were of equal height. Neither could have been over four feet.

Were there purple fireflies in ancient Egypt? Those twinkling lights ... Jagger shook his head; his imagination was on overdrive.

The woman glanced back at the two men then turned

to the audience of sailors, staring at her with dangling jaws. She flaunted a sardonic smile, one eyebrow cocked high. She looked like she was in her early twenties and wore a gauzy gown that glittered in the sunlight. Gold strands hung from her ears and neck, and golden sandals wound up her legs to her knees. Thick, black hair fell to her shoulders in small braids.

"Mut," she announced, as if her name said it all, like she was Beyoncé. "My companions are Hemet and Mutef." She whirled a polished finger at her sidekicks.

"Mutbenret!" The captain beamed. "I didn't expect you."

"No, nor did I," the prince quipped, frowning.

"I do like to surprise." Her eyes pulsed when she said it. Her glance danced over the ship's deck, dawdling briefly on Aria, then Jagger.

Jagger's muscles tensed. He scanned the dock, expecting to see Scrawny and Brawny. Had they sent this woman? Did she work for the General? Was the General out there, watching them right now?

"She's like a talking doll," Aria breathed. "Her name is moot? Like moot point?"

Jagger shook his head, too confused to help his sister pronounce moot.

"Hello, my prince." Mut smiled at Smenkare, eyes twinkling. "Always a pleasure to be in your presence."

"Mutbenret." The prince nodded. His lips were tight.

"New friends?" Her perfectly arched eyebrow inched up as she turned brown eyes, meticulously lined with kohl, on Jagger and Aria.

"Not really." The prince's voice cracked, and he scowled. "I'm just doing my royal duty, taking care of my people, showing them to their quarters and such." He put a hand on Jagger's shoulder, driving him forward. "We wouldn't want them to get lost, trying to find their way."

Moving toward the barn-like structure, Jagger craned his neck to look back at the woman. She leaned into the captain, whispering, as the prince steered he and Aria into the rectangular building on the back of the ship, down narrow steps, and into a small cabin with two cots and a wooden chest, nailed to the ground.

"But …" Jagger paused just inside the small room. "Are we captives?"

"Don't be silly, Jaaaagggggger." Smenkare drew out Jagger's name, smirking. "You asked where you were staying. I'm showing you. You're free to move about the ship. After all," the prince said, as one side of his mouth lifted, leaving the other side behind. "Where would you go?" He shut the door, leaving Jagger alone with his sister for the first time since she touched the *ankh*.

"Maybe *she's* the Protector." Aria's eyes were wide as she slid down onto the cot.

Jagger ran his hands over his fuzzy head—his missing

curls were almost as bothersome as his sister's naiveté. "Is there anyone you *don't* trust?"

Aria cocked her head to the side, then shrugged. "I think that was magic she did when those two guys jumped. It's like they were riding the wind. And Tatia said the Protector was magical. Plus, Moot Point smelled like lotus blossoms."

"Aaaaand … that's important because?" Honestly, mathematical physics was easier to understand than his sister's thought processes.

"Yeah, you're right." She tapped her cheek with one finger. "It's probably him. He saved us, and he's obviously helping us get away from the evil stink-bug General. He's taking us to Thebes. Plus, he's Tatia's brother."

"That doesn't mean we can trust him." Jagger eyeballed the door, wondering if the prince was listening to them from the other side.

"Well it sort of does. I mean, he's her *brother*."

Jagger fell onto the other cot, dropping his face in his hands. "Not all brothers are good guys. Families are weird." He peeked at her through his fingers. "Look at us." He swallowed an inexplicable urge to giggle. He couldn't believe this was actually happening.

"We're not weird." Aria sat crisscross applesauce, resting her elbows on her knees.

Jagger dropped his hands and stared at her. "Seriously? Have you met us?" His sister insisted on pretending their family was normal, like being ignored by their father and raised by a single mother across seven continents was no big deal.

"Whatever." She rolled her eyes. "Besides, what's so weird about their family? I mean, aside from the fact that they're royal. And have a lot of kids."

Jagger nodded—this topic was more comfortable. "The king and queen have five girls. We've now seen all of the princesses. And the king has two sons with other wives: Tut, who we saw at the palace, and Smenkare, who you think we should trust even though he kidnapped us less than an hour ago."

"Other wives?" Aria's eyes opened wide.

Jagger shrugged. "Egyptian kings got away with stuff."

"What about the queens?"

"They got away with less."

"That's unfair." Aria scowled.

"Yeah, lil' sis." He almost grinned. Aria was always on the lookout for inequities, real and imagined. "But the real shocker here is that Akhenaten's daughter doesn't worship the Aten."

"So what?" Aria struggled to free a curl from her braids. "We have every religion imaginable in Chicago. Remember that time I went to a Mormon church, a synagogue, and a mosque in one week? Can't Egyptians decide what church to go to too?"

"It's not like that here." Jagger shook his head. "Egyptians all believed there were loads of gods, until Akhenaten forced the Aten on them," he explained. "Different people might have had different favorites. Like if you were a scribe, you might favor the scribal god, Thoth. Or sometimes people worshipped specific gods because of stuff going on in their lives. Like there would be one god you'd go to for bad teeth, and a different god for your crush—like the one you had on Ellis last year—and another god to help people make money. And there were lots of different kinds of gods: child gods and animal gods. They even had a tree goddess that was half tree, half knock-out."

Aria giggled. "Well I guess if you were a god, you could be whatever you wanted to be. I think I'd be a panther … or maybe an owl," she said with a grin. "A girl god would be awesome—"

"Egyptians had loads of goddesses. But Tatia's dad made everyone worship his sun god. At least, I thought he did." Jagger rolled onto his stomach, dangling his elbows off the end of the cot. It smelled like fish.

"Why do you know so much about this place? I mean all those history books you read," she said as she scrunched her nose. "Aren't they boring?"

"You say boring. I'd say safe. It beats travelling through time, facing an evil General who wants to wipe out our entire family. I wish I were home reading right now. On our sofa.

With a fat slice of Chicago deep-dish pizza."

"Giordo's," she quipped.

"Louie's," he corrected her, as he had many times before. Everyone knew Louie's had the best Chicago deep-dish.

Jagger's stomach ached at the thought of pizza. He rolled toward the wall, longing for home, and they both fell silent.

"Think Mom knows we're gone yet?" Aria's voice was low.

The thought was like a kick in the gut. Jagger had been trying not to think about how upset Mom would be when she realized they'd disappeared. Would she know it was his fault?

"Maybe," he admitted after a pause. "But who knows? Maybe we'll get back, and it will be one minute after we left. It *is* time travel. Weirder things have happened. Oh, wait!" He banged his head against his knuckles. "What am I saying? Nothing weirder than this has ever happened in the entire history of the world."

"Jagger!" Aria hissed. She stared at the door, eyes wide. She sniffed, then tapped her nose. "Lotus blossoms," she whispered.

Jagger jumped up, heart thumping. He tiptoed to the door and yanked it open.

Mut stood outside, arms folded, staring at him. A mischievous smile played around her lips. One of her guards stood behind her. "Senet?" she asked.

"Senet," Jagger repeated, stalling for time. Senet was a

popular board game. That much he knew. He'd seen game pieces in museums, but he didn't have a clue how to play it.

"Come." She tipped her head toward the stairs. "I'll teach you. No fun being stuck in a ..." She looked around the small room. "Here." She grimaced.

"Okay!" Aria jumped off the cot and bounced out the door, following the ancient beauty up the short flight of steps into the sunlight.

Jagger sighed, then trailed them.

The Senet lesson was the first of many. The gameplay was simple enough, but Jagger was too busy trying to figure out who was trying to save them and who was trying to kill them to focus. Aria picked it up quicker than him, which stung.

The next two days passed like a dream he couldn't wake up from. He and Aria spent most of their time on deck, playing Senet with Mut and Smenkare, sometimes the captain. They played for hours under a shade umbrella on top of the barn-like building, snacking on bread slathered in honey and date tarts the first mate brought them. It wasn't deep-dish, but it didn't suck.

Jagger tried to tease information out of Mut and the prince, but it was useless. It didn't help that he was never alone with either of them. If Smenkare was playing, Mut or one of her sidekicks was within earshot. If Mut played, the prince loitered nearby. Babi came and went, jovial but guarded. Neither of Mut's guards uttered a word, even when Aria tried to charm them. Jagger wasn't entirely sure they *could* talk.

The lack of sleep made everything worse. He knew ancient Egyptians used wooden pillows inscribed with sleep spells, but he'd never given any thought to just how uncomfortable wooden pillows could be.

Sometimes Mut flirted with the prince, even though he was about a decade her junior. She tossed her braided wig, touched Smenkare's shoulder, and laughed at nearly everything he said, which was particularly noteworthy, as the prince had *no* sense of humor. If her bids to beguile him worked, Smenkare hid it well.

The prince's mask only slipped once over the two long days.

The afternoon of their second day aboard, Aria and Mut were playing while Jagger watched the shore speed by, thinking of Gramps. Gramps would sit by Lake Michigan for hours, a pole in his hand and a smile on his face, while Jagger did homework by his side. Gramps didn't even care if he caught a fish. He just loved sitting in the sun, watching it play on the water. Jagger's eyes stung as he watched a boy lead a herd of sheep along the shore as two old men cast fishing nets into the water. One second the scene was in front of him. The next, it was behind him.

"Wait." Jagger stared back at the shrinking men. "How fast are we going?" He turned to ask the captain, but Babi was gone.

"Hmmm." The prince straightened and turned to Mut. "An interesting question." His eyes narrowed on her as he tapped steepled fingers together. The guard standing sentry behind Mut shifted closer to her.

Jagger stared back to the shore, calculating their speed in his head. He glanced up at the sail, full of wind. Too full. Sure, he felt wind against his skin, but not that much wind. Were those more purple fireflies, stuck in the sail? What was happening here?

"It's magic." Aria clapped, gazing adoringly at the white sail fluttering in the wind. "You?" She looked at Mut. "Or …" She shifted her gaze to Smenkare.

Mut's smile was as enigmatic as the sphinx, but the prince was stone-faced.

"Wait. So how long until we get to Thebes?" Jagger asked, rubbing the letter still stuffed in his kilt's inside pocket. If they could get to Thebes, they could get to Herihor, the one guy Jagger knew they could trust. He'd assumed they had three more days on the ship, but at this speed …

He felt Smenkare's glare boring into him and looked up at him. The prince looked away.

"Not long." Mut smiled. "Not long at all."

The attack came the next morning.

9

WHAT THE CROC?

*B*ang!

"What's happening?" Aria squeezed the rail so tight her knuckles faded to white.

"I don't know." Jagger leaned over the river, searching for danger. Water splashed off to the left, and he fought a sudden urge to pee.

Mut rushed up and grabbed Jagger's arm. "Where's the prince?"

Jagger shook his head, confused. "I don't—"

"We haven't seen him." Aria scanned the deck.

"The amulet, Jagger!" Mut yanked on the leather strap hanging from Jagger's neck just as the captain strode up, Mut's two guards at his side. "You must find Smenkare."

"Wait. How did you know about—". Jagger's mind felt as cluttered as Aria's closet.

"You *are* the Protector!" Aria bounced up and down.

"Yes, Aria." Mut spared her a small smile. "Now, Jagger."

"Yay!" Aria beamed. "You were my first choice. I like you much more than him—"

"It's not a reality show!" Jagger shouted. "We're under attack."

Bang!

The ship reeled, as if to emphasize his point.

"What's happening?" Jagger turned back to the water churning beneath the ship.

"Damage assessment. Now!" The captain's voice was steady. Soldiers scurried at his command.

"Find Smenkare!" Mut urged Jagger, jingling the Isis Knot.

"Yeah. Okay." *Breathe*. He gulped air and clutched the amulet, focusing his thoughts on the prince. He'd used the amulet a few times since he'd been on the ship, feeling sheepish at first as he concentrated on Tatia, sensing her recede in the distance. He'd even tried Mom, but nothing happened. The prince's presence, however, stood out like a beacon. "He's in front of us, maybe ten kilometers, near the shore." Jagger pointed.

"And your letter of introduction?" Mut pressed her hands to her temples. Hemet and Mutef stood behind her, stern faced as always.

"My …" Jagger dropped the amulet, grabbing the pocket where he'd kept Tatia's letter to Herihor. "It's … Wait! How?"

Mut put her hands on his shoulders. "I suspect Smenkare took it," she said. "But certainty is always wise." She nodded at the amulet.

"Right," Jagger mumbled. "Okay. Right." He squeezed his eyes shut tight. His palm, wrapped tightly around the amulet, was slick with sweat. He concentrated on the letter, and moaned when it came into focus. "Smenkare has it."

"And my magic kit too, I suspect." Mut sighed. "I'm a magician without a bag of tricks now. I'm not sure how we'll get you in to see the High Priest without Meretaten's letter. It's impossible to reach Herihor in his temple fortress. The man is a hermit!"

BANG! The ship lurched to one side, then the other.

"I think we have a more immediate problem," the captain said coolly, eyeballing the Nile. Mut pivoted and leaned over the rail beside him.

BANG! BANG!

Jagger's stomach rolled with the lurching ship. Peering over Mut's shoulder, he struggled to believe his eyes.

Giant crocodiles!

There were several of them, sharp teeth gleaming under blood red eyes. The scales on their backs were spiky—long daggers shooting from their spines. They were the size of the small yachts that sailed Lake Michigan. Jagger tried to count them, but they moved too fast, diving, surfacing, and twining around one another.

"I've never seen anything like this." Babi's voice was calm, but his brows were furrowed.

"And you probably never will again." Mut's eyes were wide. She looked more fascinated than scared. "Those are the crocs of Sobek, the god of war. They only appear if summoned by a fairly powerful magician. Smenkare must have called them before he left. Apparently, the prince's magical abilities are stronger than I'd assumed. If only I had my magic kit." She sighed.

BANG, BANG, BANG!

At this rate, the ship would tip over any minute. The guy next to Jagger whispered under his breath: a protection spell, Jagger realized. He looked around. Sailors were clutching amulets and chanting to the gods.

Even Aria looked worried, grasping the ship's rail, jaw hanging open as she watched the crocs squirm through the water. She looked too pale, like she did after a bad asthma attack.

"Can you defeat them?" Babi asked Mut.

"I could if I had my magic kit." She bit her bottom lip. "Without it …" She shook her head.

"What would you do if you had it?" Jagger had no idea how shooting questions at her would help, but his brain was accustomed to clicking through possibilities, sorting solutions from dead ends.

"I need wax." She glanced at the captain.

Babi shook his head. "We have tar to fix, well, breaks like the ones we're getting right now. Would that help?"

BANG!

"No. That won't do." She grimaced, curving her long neck to watch one of the oversized crocs twine its body around the ship's hull.

BANG!

"Tar has the wrong properties," she continued. "I need raw material, something void of magical properties that I can shape to my will, something that's not already imbued with the power of the old gods. I need to call on Neith, goddess of war and the waters of creation. Only her magic can trump Sobek's crocs. Fortunately, I know the spell. Unfortunately, I need wax from my magic kit to cast it."

BANG, BANG!

"What would you do exactly? If you had wax?" Jagger's brain was churning, looking for solutions. He tried to put Aria out of his mind. Having her two steps from death's door was distracting.

"I need to create a wax Apep to cast the spell."

Aria's face scrunched up in confusion.

"Apep is a giant snake," Jagger explained. "A symbol of chaos. Neith was his mom too. She was a pretty powerful goddess with some unusual kids."

"So we need a giant snake to kill the giant crocodiles?" Aria wrinkled her nose then shrugged. "That makes sense. How much wax do you need?"

BANG! BANG!

The ship tipped. Men and boxes slid to one side of the deck. The captain grabbed Mut with one hand, holding her tight as he grasped the rail with his other. One of Mut's guards grabbed her waist but the other fell to the deck.

BANG!

The ship rocked again. Jagger and Aria went spinning. He managed to grab onto a rope with one hand and his sister's wrist with the other as they slid down the tilted deck. He heard a splash and hoped a box, rather than a sailor, just went overboard. He hated to think of what those crocs would do if they managed to get someone between those fierce teeth.

Aria's arms slipped down his sweaty palm, and he squeezed her tighter. The ship righted itself just in time—a second more and she'd have slithered away. Jagger and Aria landed in a heap on the deck.

Aria crawled toward Mut. "How much wax do you need?"

"Not much. I need enough to craft a snake, and I need a few arrows."

"Arrows we have." The captain ordered a nearby sailor to bring arrows. Thinking he wanted to drive off the crocs, sailors started shooting at them.

"That won't work," Mut said casually, as if she were

turning down a pair of new shoes.

"What about …" With a squeal, Aria pulled her sparkly, purple purse from under her shift. She shuffled through it and extracted a handful of small, silver rectangles along with a pink box.

She tossed the box at Jagger. "Think it will work?"

It took him a moment to understand what his sister was up to. "No! No, I don't."

"That's 'cause you're a Pauly Pessimist," Aria retorted, shoving a pink stick in her mouth.

BANG!

He tensed, then relented. "Let's see if she likes spearmint or bubblegum, I guess." He scrabbled over to his sister, chewing a huge wad of gum as quickly as possible.

BANG!

Mut watched them, head cocked to one side, as Babi directed sailors. Mutef and Hemet stood at her back—their the-world-is-ending faces looked exactly like their it's-lovely-outside-today faces.

Jagger and Aria handed Mut their gobs of quickly chewed gum.

She squeezed it, then pulled it. A smile spread slowly across her face. "I can use this!" she breathed. "It's so … blank! It's *unnatural*. It has no divine properties at all."

She slid to her knees, rolling the chewed gum between both hands. She laid the small, gummy snake she'd crafted on the deck and covered it with two crossed arrows, snatched from a sailor who was uselessly shooting at the crocs. She was waggling her fingers and chanting, "Come, Neith the Mother, Neith the Warrior, Neith the Protector ..." Purple lights twinkled around like fairies in dresses, ranging from violet to maroon. Aria wiggled her nose dramatically, and Jagger realized the air smelled like lotus.

"She's doing magic." Aria elbowed Jagger. How could she smile at a time like this?

BANG.

Jagger held his breath.

TTTHHHHHHHUUUUMMPP!

Okay. That sound was new.

Mut jumped up and ran to the rail, hanging over to stare down at the water. The captain, Jagger, and Aria rushed to her side. Jagger shoved himself between Aria and one of Mut's guards.

Nothing. The water was still.

TTHHHUUUMMP! TTTHHHUUUMP!

The head of a gargantuan snake reared up, holding a croc between its teeth. Its scales were the size of a small house, glimmering yellow. Huge, black spots ran along its enormous back, and two long fangs protruded from its mouth. The croc looked small, sandwiched between them.

The snake gazed at Mut, its yellow eyes whirling. Like a dog releasing a dead rat at its owner's feet, it dropped the bloody croc, and spun toward the next one.

TTTTHHHUUUUUMMP!

"Well," Mut said dryly, following the snake with her eyes. "I've not only underestimated the prince's powers, but his ambition as well. Clearly he's the one working with the General."

Jagger shook his head, struggling to process the last ten minutes. How was it possible for his crazy life to get even crazier?

"Smenkare is trying to kill his own family?" Aria hunched up like a cat.

"And ours!" Jagger added. His sister seemed to forget their lives were at stake too.

Mut quirked a brow. "It wouldn't be the first time someone in the family has murdered in pursuit of the crown. Although I'll admit, I wouldn't have pegged Smenkare as a killer. A whiner, yes. A murderer ... well, that's a surprise."

"But ..." Jagger fumbled. "Won't he die too? Tatia said if the General casts the spell, the entire family will die. *He's* family!"

Mut tapped her fingers against the rail. "Yes. That's a puzzle that needs solving."

TTHHUUUMMP!

The snake gave the water one last whack as it disappeared under the waves, crocs devoured. The ship was eerily silent. Everyone on deck stared out at the Nile, holding their collective breath, hoping it was really over.

Nothing but peace and calm, as if they hadn't almost been eaten by giant crocodiles and saved by an even more giant snake.

Jagger watched the river banks as the ship floated serenely along, feeling stunned and scared and, above all, intimidated. He'd faced real danger for the first time in his life, and he'd done nothing remotely useful. Why on earth did Tatia—and the old gods, if the princess was to be believed—think he could do this? Even his little sister had outperformed him. He'd have never thought to grab handfuls of gum. Maybe the gods had meant for the princess to summon Aria. Thinking of his sister, Jagger turned to her. "You okay?"

She grinned, eyes sparkling. Leave it to Aria to believe magical beasts were the coolest thing ever … even when they were trying to kill you! "That was even more interesting than the tiger that chased us when Mom took us on safari, or the time you got food poisoning in Istanbul!"

Jagger sighed. His sister had a bad habit of confusing danger with adventure.

"I guess this means the easy part is over, huh?" Aria leaned her elbows on the rail. "Soon we'll be in Thebes. We'll have to, I don't know, do something."

Jagger stared at his little sister, thinking he should compliment her on her quick thinking but worried she'd realize he was useless if he voiced the fact that she'd saved the day while he froze.

Aria rolled her eyes. "No, Brainy. I'm really not a total idiot. I have no idea why you think you're the only one who can do things! Hopefully your faith in your own oversized brain means you have some kind of plan?"

"A plan?" Jagger replied. Of course he didn't have a plan. With a sigh, he confessed, "No, I don't have a plan. I mean, I guess the plan was to get to Herihor and hope he knew what to do. But how are we going to do that now?"

Aria scowled. "Smell-kare is a butthead. Tatia gave *you* the letter!"

Jagger shut his tingly eyes. "I keep hoping I'll wake up and realize I'm still in our rental house in Amarna. Mom will be making coffee, and you'll be talking to Grams on the phone, probably complaining about me making you do math on the plane."

Aria melted, flashing a sympathetic smile as she patted his back.

"It's like we're in an alternate universe," he continued. "I mean, I thought I understood ancient Egypt. Sure, I knew some people believed in magic—their doctors performed magic spells along with real cures—but I didn't think there really *was* magic. It's like the entire world is different from what I thought it was. And I thought I understood the world, how it worked, the science behind it all."

"What happened to 'Einstein said we could travel through time?'"

"Yeah, but he didn't say some necklace could tell me where stuff was, or that a few pieces of gum and a magic spell could ward off oversized crocodiles!"

"I know, right?" Aria smiled, delighted by the same mysteries that Jagger found downright depressing. "Look on the bright side. We're with the Protector now. I mean, she's not as muscle-y as I'd imagined, but she's way more fabulous. She'll help us. And we're almost at Thebes, which is exactly where Tatia wanted us to go. Plus, we survived a croc attack. We're lucky, if you think about it the right way."

Jagger looked over at Mut, flanked by Hemet and Mutef, whispering with the captain. Babi looked calm. Did this guy ever get ruffled? Maybe he was in on it. Maybe he knew the croc attack was going to happen, so he wasn't actually surprised.

Mut must have felt Jagger's eyes on them. She turned and strode toward them. Three graceful steps later, she straightened Aria's crooked headband with a tight smile. "Well." Her grin flagged. "That was unexpected."

The captain, in her wake, chuckled. "That's one word for it."

"But, but," Jagger stuttered. "How are we going to get Herihor's help without Tatia's letter of introduction?"

"Yes." Mut threw her shoulders back. "That puzzle we must solve immediately."

10

PARADING WITH KHONS-WHO?

"My quarters," the captain said to Mut, nodding at Jagger and Aria to follow.

Moments later, the four of them sat around a rectangular table in the captain's cozy office. Hemet and Mutef stood at attention behind Mut's chair.

"About your bag of magic," the captain began.

Mut waved off his concern. "I can replenish in Thebes."

"I was talking to her." Babi nodded at Aria, who hugged her bag to her chest like it was her most prized stuffed animal, a floppy-eared, yellow bunny Dad gave her on the only Easter they ever spent with him. She'd dragged that thing across the planet ten times over.

"Right." Mut flashed a lopsided grin, considering Aria

and her sparkly, purple purse. "That was impressive. Any chance there's something in there that can replace the letter of introduction Smenkare stole so we can get you two in to see Herihor?"

Aria cocked her head to the side, then shook it. "No ancient scrolls, sorry."

"Maybe it's time I get the whole story." The captain drummed his fingers on the table.

Mut bit her lip. "You know some of it already," she admitted. "What you don't know—"

"Wait …" Jagger leaned forward. "How do we know …" He swallowed hard. He wasn't entirely sure he should trust Mut. But she knew about the letter and the Isis Knot amulet. How would she have known that stuff if she *wasn't* the Protector? But Tatia hadn't said anything about the captain. "I mean …"

Mut reached a flawless hand across the table and laid it on his fidgeting fingers. "I'd trust Babi with my life," she said. "And right now, I'm going to trust him with yours. Because we need a new plan. And new plans benefit from new allies."

Jagger looked at Aria.

She rolled her eyes. "He's not Dad either," she pouted.

He stared down at his dirty fingernails, feeling their eyes on him. He wasn't convinced, but what choice did he have? He shrugged.

Mut spared Jagger a patient grin before turning back to

Babi. Jagger watched the captain through hooded eyes as Mut told him about Mek's *Ka* and Tatia's actions and the General's plans. Babi's eyes grew wider as the tale progressed.

"So I'm here to help Jagger find the gemstones that house Mek's *Ka* before the spell is cast," Mut concluded. "And, if the gods are kind, to return them before she dies so she can enjoy her much-deserved afterlife."

"That's quite a tale." Babi leaned back, scowling. "The General must be in Thebes. And now he'll know the three of you are near." He rubbed his stubbly cheek. "And that you're headed for Herihor."

"The good news is we know who's helping him." Mut snuggled into her chair. "Smenkare isn't the strongest magician—the *Heqa-oo Moot* seems beyond his abilities. He's also not much of a brother. But I wouldn't have suspected him of murdering his half-sisters, or Tut. Although his father, well, that's no surprise—Smenkare detests Pharaoh. And Nefertiti."

"That kid has a history of bad choices." Babi rapped his knuckles on the table and huffed. "Step one is to get Jagger and Aria in front of the High Priest." His eyes found Mut's. "Sounds like a job for a good smuggler."

"Know any?" Mut raised a brow, her lips hinting at a smile.

"Oh, I know a guy. Toss in a brilliant magician, two fearless guards, and a couple of kids with a bag full of mystery items, and we might just get to Herihor without that letter.

But how?" He paused and the tap, tap, tap of his fingers against the table irked Jagger. "Today is festival day, so Thebes will be more crowded than usual—"

"Festival day?" Jagger leaned forward. "A religious festival?"

Babi nodded.

"Festival day," Jagger mused softly. All eyes were on him. He dropped his head back against the chair and pressed his hands to his face. Eyes shut tight, he imagined the books and articles he'd read about ancient Egyptian, religious festivals. There was something ... *temples, statues, food, dancing, priests, floats, incense ...* He teased out the memory, and his head snapped up.

He froze. His eyes shifted to Babi. What if ...?

"Spill it, Brainy." Aria crossed her arms over her chest.

Jagger's grip tightened on the arms of his chair. "I guess ... maybe ..." What if he was wrong?

"Just say it," Aria chided.

He sighed. "Okay. I do have one idea. It might be a ridiculous, crazy, absurd idea. But it's an idea."

A few hours later, having explored purse, pockets, the ship's hull, and Jagger's knowledge of ancient religious festivals, they had a plan.

Aria was decked out in Mut's fanciest jewel-encrusted tunic. Jagger stood next to her, dressed as a priest of Amun-Ra, in a white, linen kilt with gold armbands circling his biceps. He dabbed at the kohl around his eyes. He was getting used to the makeup, but not his hair—he ran his hand over his head, missing his 'fro.

Nearby, Hemet and Mutef were squirming into wooden barrels. Babi watched the recently dumped wine turn the Nile red as he strapped a royal soldier's leather chest guard over his pecs.

"Dock when the pier is busy," Babi told his second-in-command. "We want everyone to see Mut and her barrels disembark. And don't be shy making your way to the Workman's Village. The more convinced Smenkare and the General are that Jagger and Aria were smuggled into the Village, the more likely we are to succeed. So make some noise in there." He gave Hemet a playful sock in the arm.

"Good luck, Captain." Mut stared deeply into Babi's eyes, and Jagger squirmed. Just how well did these two know each other? Mut turned and pulled Aria in for a hug.

"Wait." Jagger stepped back when she whirled toward him. "Maybe Babi should go with Mutef and Hemet, and we should stay with you."

Mut and Babi exchanged a glance.

"Good grief, Brainy," Aria moaned. "We've gone over this a hundred times. Smell-kare and the General will assume we'll stick to Mut like glue. Because she's the Protector. And the magician. That's why we're going with Babi. Do we need to say it slower so your big brain can process it?"

Jagger shifted his weight back and forth. What if Babi took them straight to the General? Arguments thundered through his head. Too slowly. His sister jumped into a rowboat with Babi and two sailors. With a heavy sigh, Jagger followed her. He pouted as the sailors sped them toward the shore.

Babi sat across from Jagger on the boat's small bench, tapping his fingers on his knees. His eyes stuck to Jagger like a magnet to ferromagnetic material. "You'll see, kid." He shrugged. "I never abandon my friends."

Jagger's spine stiffened. "We're not friends." He rubbed his almost-bald head as a smile spread across the captain's face. Babi glanced over at an annoyed looking Aria and winked. She rolled her eyes at him conspiratorially then stared down at the river as if she could spear a fish with her gaze.

A few minutes later, they landed on the outskirts of town. The sailors pulled the rowboat into a nearby field and hid it under stalky, yellow vegetation, then Babi led them through farms toward the city center. They plodded past hovels of mud brick and dirty kids carrying vegetables from a field.

"So the gods need rides, and the priests are like Chicago cabbies?" Aria quizzed Jagger as they reached the city outskirts and trekked past small homes and vendors and busy people.

Jagger curled his hands into fists, exhausted by his sister's cluelessness. "Not sure I've ever heard a ride with a Chicago cabbie described as religious experience, but sort of. I guess. Gold statues of the gods are hidden in small huts on top of floats. The priests pull them from temple to temple so the gods can visit each other." Jagger couldn't ignore the stirring of intellectual curiosity. He'd read about the festivals. And now he was going to see one!

"The gods have playdates at each other's houses," Aria said as if it were the most logical thing ever. "And they need a ride. That tracks."

Jagger scowled, but Babi laughed, deep in his belly.

Jagger was formulating a riveting history-laden response in his head, when the view transformed. An enormous temple loomed before them, stretching to the sky. Jagger stopped in his tracks, gazing up at the white, sandstone walls that surrounded the temple. The walls were covered in vibrant reliefs. Images of larger-than-life gods were besieged by colorful hieroglyphs. Tall, crimson flags flapped in the wind at the temple's towering, front entrance.

"Come on." Babi ushered them toward the back of the crowd.

Aria rubbed sweat off her face with a corner of her cloak.

She and Babi hid their costumes under linen cloaks. Jagger and the sailors fit right in—they looked like all the other priests roaming around.

Jagger followed, clutching the amulet. "Mut, Mutef, and Hemet are on the shore."

"Good." The captain nodded. "They'll be at the dock. Now, we go this way." Babi led them behind the crowd, walking parallel to the wide boulevard toward the larger temple barely visible at the far end of a long, sphinx-lined avenue. "Most people will stay near the two larger temples to see the god, Amun-Ra, his wife, Mut, and their son, Khonsu. The kid has his own float, and that's the one we want. The way-stations between the temples will be less crowded. The free bread and beer are at the temples, not to mention the dancers and acrobats."

Jagger's stomach did a somersault at the smell of meat and spices mingling in the air.

They approached a stone sphinx, larger than the others, surrounded by a scattering of people. An old woman in rags, missing most of her teeth, was selling fertility amulets. The words flying from her mouth made Jagger want to cover Aria's ears.

"Khonsu's float will stop here," Babi whispered before directing the two soldiers to take up positions in the sparse crowd. "Be ready."

One by one, the first two large floats—made of gold,

Lebanese cedar, and precious stones—passed by, accompanied by priests and priestesses. A priest wearing a ram's head led the procession. The huts, hiding the gods inside, jiggled with each step as the priestesses rattled loud instruments. Each float paused briefly as it reached the sphinx, and the priests set their heavy burden down on nearby brackets that held the float about a foot above ground, protecting it from the dirt. As the float rested, the sparse crowd fell to their knees in adoration. The priests performed some kind of ritual that involved a lot of noise and some very smelly incense, but Jagger guessed they really just needed a rest from carrying the heavy floats.

The two floats, and their entourages, moved on after the ceremonies were done, and another float appeared. Although every bit as flashy as the first two, with a huge, golden crescent moon affixed to the top, Khonsu's float had fewer priests accompanying it. A mere eight men carried the float, accompanied by a scattering of priestesses.

As with Amun-Ra and Mut's floats, the priests set Khonsu's float down on the nearby brackets, and the crowd fell to its collective knees.

"It's time," Babi whispered to Jagger and Aria.

Jagger ground his teeth, waiting.

Pop!

He blew out a puff of air.

Pop! Pop!

The crowd gasped. People turned in circles, searching for the source of the unfamiliar sound.

Pop. Pop. Pop!

Babi tossed off his cloak and shouted commands. "Take cover. Get to the temple."

People started running, scared. More Chinese poppers, left over from the kids' last visit to Chicago's Chinatown and mined from Aria's purse, burst. Babi's soldiers were dropping them as they ran along with the crowd, herding people away from the float.

"You too," Babi yelled at the priests. "Get to the temple."

Most did as bid, but a few brave souls stayed to protect their god, as Babi had predicted.

"Now," he whispered to Aria.

Jagger's stomach was in knots as she wiggled out of her cloak and walked toward the remaining priests. Her lips were pursed in her I-mean-business look. Jagger rushed to keep up.

"Bow for your princess." Babi's voice carried authority.

A few of the priests dropped instantly, but several stood gawking.

"I said bow," Babi repeated.

All but one hit the ground.

Aria turned to face the man who stayed on his feet. "I'm sorry to interrupt you, but I've come a very long way, from the city of Amarna, to meet your god, Khons-who. I'm sure you can understand." She added her I'm-so-sweet smile and batted her lashes. "That it's difficult for me to show myself, under the circumstances."

"You're the princess?" the priest stammered. "Our princess? From Amarna? And you want to talk to Khonsu?"

"Our princess insisted we accompany her here for the festival." Babi leaned toward the priest, speaking lowly. "She adores the old gods, but she's dedicated to Khonsu above all. This must remain secret. Her life would be in danger if the Aten's forces learned of her loyalty. We trust you to keep this to yourselves, but she begs a moment alone with your god. This loyal priest of Amun-Ra," he said as he motioned toward Jagger. "Has accompanied her from Amarna. He'll attend her as she devotes herself to Khonsu. Privately."

"A priest of Amun-Ra? From Amarna?" The priest's eyes bulged like a cartoon character as he stared at Jagger. "I didn't think ... How is that ..."

Jagger cleared his throat. He was amazed at Aria's brazenness. She played the part like a Hollywood starlet. This princess thing must be going to her head! Determined not to be outdone by his little sister again, he stood taller. "It's dangerous. But we ... we keep the worship of the old gods strong in the new city. The princess is ... is one of our most devoted believers."

"Truly?" The priest's eye softened.

Jagger almost felt sorry for the guy. He looked genuinely

touched as he wiped wet eyes and motioned the others to stand. "Of course, we'll give her a moment. Bless you, princess."

"Your loyalty is appreciated," Babi soothed him as he gestured for the priest and his men to turn away, steering them down the street and nodding at Jagger to move quickly.

Adrenaline coursed through Jagger as he waited for the priests to leave. A few feet away, the priest turned back and stared at Aria. "Did you make that awful noise?"

Aria froze. She glanced at Jagger. He shook his head, pointing slyly at the float.

"No," she replied smoothly. "That was Khons-who, helping me in my quest."

"Khons*u*," Jagger whispered under his breath.

The guy fanned himself. At Babi's prompting, he turned and waddled away.

Jagger jerked back the float's curtain, revealing the god's statue: a solid gold child, dressed in a linen kilt with gems hanging from his ears and neck and a silver moon atop his head. Khonsu sat on a plush bench, filling the hut's space. No room there. And the statue was too heavy to move. Where would they hide a statue worth a fortune anyway? Not exactly a plan designed to avoid attention.

Jagger yanked the curtain back in place and dropped to the ground, wriggling under the float. "Be here," he mumbled to himself.

Yes! A false door, just as he'd hoped. Babi and Mut were surprised when Jagger told them the floats had hidden compartments, designed for a priest to hide in so they could speak to the crowd in the god's voice. He heaved a sigh of relief. Their entire plan had rested on his book knowledge of ancient float construction. And over the past few days, Jagger had learned that the facts he'd gathered from books weren't as reliable as he'd always assumed.

Opening the small trap door, Jagger flashed his phone light around the human-sized space. He pulled out a bag, and Aria pushed it behind the stone sphinx.

"Hurry." He helped his sister in first, then crawled in behind her and wiggled the door shut. It was a tight fit. He and Aria were shoved together like sardines in the cans Grams kept in the back of her cupboard. When he turned off his flashlight, it was pitch black. Aria's breathing sounded thunderous.

"You okay?" he whispered, cursing himself for not keeping her inhaler handy.

"Sshh," she shot back.

The next few minutes dragged on. Babi and the priests finally returned, and Jagger heard the clinking sounds of the captain handing over Mut's gold. Then, the float was lifted, and they began moving. Something sharp dug into Jagger's side as the float swayed back and forth.

Jagger bit his lip, holding in the moan that threatened to escape. This was going to be a long, hard, jet-black ride.

11

TEMPLE RUN

Jagger and Aria bumped along in the dark for what seemed like hours. Her skin felt wet and clammy against his. Worse, her breath was ragged. What if her asthma was reaching the danger zone? He wanted to ask her, but the priests carrying the float were so close he could hear them panting from exertion.

Jagger tried to distract himself, tracking the whereabouts of Mut and Babi with his amulet: she was across the Nile with Hemet and Mutef, but the captain was sticking by the float as the procession moved to the small temple then headed back the way it had come, toward the larger temple of Amun-Ra.

Mostly, Jagger fretted. What if Aria's asthma spiraled? What would happen if they didn't find Herihor? What would

Jagger say if they did find the High Priest? He concocted speeches in his mind, designed to convince the priest to help them. Jagger could only hope Herihor would know what to do … *if* they managed to find the guy.

Finally, the sounds of the crowd faded. They must be entering the large temple. Egyptian temples were built like long corridors. The large, front areas were open to all worshippers, but the holy of holies, the deepest part of the temple, was only accessible to the highest-ranking members of the priesthood. That's where the god's statue would rest.

He flinched when the float finally sank to the floor with a thunk—a thunk followed by the sounds of receding footsteps. The silence was all encompassing after the roar of the crowds and musicians. The smells of sweat and livestock were replaced by the smells of incense and cooked meat.

Aria's fingers found his. She was slick with sweat, sniffling softly. Was she trying not to cry? That thought terrified him—Aria only cried when she was feeling sorry for someone else, like a stray dog or a bullied friend. "Can we get out now?" she moaned lowly.

"I'm trying." He shoved the door, harder, but it didn't budge. "I think the float is on the ground." His heart was racing. He needed to get his sister out of here, but the door was stuck. The float must not be on stilts like it had been at the way-station when they crawled into the trapdoor on the bottom of the float.

Their plan had been to sneak out when the holy of holies was empty and find Herihor. But now they were trapped.

Aria squirmed, shoving a hard elbow into his stomach. Jagger was relieved to hear the hiss of her inhaler.

"I'll live." The sound Aria made was part laugh, part sob. "Unless we're about to run out of oxygen."

"No," Jagger whispered back. "There's a tube connecting this space to the god's mouth. It's for—"

"Please, no history lessons now, Brainy."

Jagger sighed. *Right.*

"Shhhh," she hissed. "Someone's coming."

Jagger froze. Soft footsteps shuffled their way. They stopped just in front of the float. A man's voice began chanting melodiously. "Hail to thee, Khonsu, Mighty Traveler, Protector ..."

Jagger's mind whirled. On one hand, he was worried about his sister. Maybe he should scream at the top of his lungs so the priest would get them out. But what if the guy was working with the General and Smenkare? For all he knew, the chanting guy was the General's favorite uncle. Mut thought that they'd be taken to Herihor if they were discovered in the temple. But what if she was wrong?

Aria's breath grew loud enough to drown out the chanting. She couldn't take much more. He knew what he had to do. But it wouldn't do her any good to be rescued then dragged back into danger.

Jagger wiggled his hand into the pocket sewn neatly into his kilt and pulled out his phone. Clicking it on, he aimed it at Aria. Black smudges marred her cheeks, the kohl so carefully drawn around her eyes now dripped from her chin. She clutched her inhaler to her cheek.

Scrolling frantically through apps, Jagger selected one he'd downloaded for a Halloween party he and Andrew hosted a few years ago. It recorded anything you said and played it back in a spooky voice. Thinking briefly, Jagger whispered into his phone. Then he held it close to the tube that was connected to the god's mouth. He hiked up the volume and pushed play.

"To whoooom are yooouu loooyaaal?" The spooky app voice was amplified by the tube.

Silence.

Jagger pushed the play button again. "To whooom are yooouu loooyaaal?"

The man cleared his throat. "I am loyal to you, my god, Khonsu. And to your parents, the illustrious Amun-Ra and your mother, Mut. My loyalty to the old gods is assured." The voice was that of an old man, but still a rich baritone.

Jagger whispered into the phone again, then pushed play.

"Aaand theee Geeeneraaaal? Can weeee cooouunt on yooouur loooyalty to the Generaalaaaalllll and theee roooyal priiiiiince?"

More silence.

Then, footsteps walked away, followed moments later by the sound of more footsteps coming back toward them. Aria's breath was so loud it was difficult to hear what was going on outside of the float.

Jagger jerked as the float was lifted. The trap door flew open, and they tumbled onto a cold, marble floor in a heap. He squinted at Aria. Sweat dripped off her as she shoved her inhaler in her mouth and gulped in a blast of albuterol. Her princess gown was destroyed, gems dangling by threads. The rich cloth that had covered her hair was a wet rag, stuck to her sandal, and dark blond curls were pasted to her face.

"Who are you?" The old man leaned down and peered at him.

Jagger recognized the voice: it was the man he'd been talking to. He wore a white kilt, and his chest was bare. In spite of his age, his body looked strong and healthy. He was bald with fuzzy eyebrows, speckled with gray.

"I asked you a question, young man." The old man stood tall and crossed his arms.

Jagger sagged. Being sneaky was exhausting. He glanced at his sister. Her breathing was normalizing. He turned back to the old man, ticking through options in his mind. Grams' voice trickled into his head: *truth is less fuss.*

"We're looking for Herihor." Jagger fidgeted. "Meretaten sent us. Our letter of introduction was, uh, lost."

The man's mouth hung open. He looked like one of the

fishes Gramps mined from the Chicago River. He leaned toward Jagger menacingly and grabbed the amulet that still hung from his neck, now sticky with sweat. After giving it a good look, the old man stood, gave Jagger a quick stare, and strode out of the room, whispering to a nearby priest before he pushed through the elaborate, golden double doors at the far end of the small chamber.

Aria and Jagger stared at each other.

Now what?

Jagger glanced around the room. It was small and white with a bright, marble floor and a gilded, gold ceiling. Khonsu's gold statue was exposed. Bowls of food sat in front of the god—the smell of food crept up Jagger's nose, triggering hunger pains.

The gold door opened with a click, and two priests stormed toward them. One grabbed Aria's arm, pulling her up. The other took hold of Jagger. The priests herded them toward the gold door. Aria threw a longing glance at the food sitting at the statue's feet, pining for the god's feast, no doubt.

The clickety-clack of their footsteps bounced off the walls as the silent priests led them through an elaborate, stone corridor. It was high and narrow, stark white. Cedar doors peppered the long stretch of pale stone. The cloying smell of incense was nearly overwhelming in the enclosed space.

Jagger wiped his clammy hands on his kilt, eyes glued to the back of Aria's head. What if Herihor wouldn't see them?

Or saw them but wouldn't help them? For all they knew, the guy was on vacation.

"Where are you taking us?" Aria must have felt as bad as she looked—she didn't even try her you-gotta-love-me smile on the priests.

It wouldn't have made a difference. Neither man uttered a word. The sound of their sandals slapping against the floor was joined by a creaking noise when the priest, who was holding his sister's arm, shoved open a door, pushed Aria inside, and slammed it shut. It happened so fast Jagger didn't have time to react.

"No!" His yell echoed down the stone hallway. "My sister …"

The priest's fingers dug deeper into his arm. The other guy opened a door, across the hall from the one Aria disappeared into, and tossed Jagger in. He was strong for a priest.

"No!" Jagger banged on the door that had crashed shut behind him. "Aria!"

"I'm here," she called back. "I'm fine. Chill!"

He should have done something to keep them together. Now they were trapped in a gigantic, stone prison, separated, and at the mercy of men who could be the General's biggest fans for all he knew!

He was yanking uselessly at his door when it flew open, and a different priest stomped in.

"My sister—"

The large priest hushed him. He pushed him gently toward a stone basin, filled with water. The small tub sat on a slab of stone at the far end of the room, simply furnished with cedar stools and chests and a few chairs covered with leather throws.

The man nodded at the basin, then pointed at an alabaster vase, sitting on a wooden stool next to it.

"You want me to clean up?" Jagger shook his head, mystified.

The man smiled, revealing three missing teeth.

"But my sister ..." Jagger argued.

The man pointed again.

Jagger eyeballed the water. "If I do this can I see my sister?"

The man's gap toothed smile grew wider.

Jagger rushed back to the door. "Aria. Are you still there?"

The pause felt eternal. "I'm fine. I think they want me to take a bath ... or a shower ... or somehow get clean. I'm goin' in. You need to relax. It's fine. I'm sure Herihor is just finishing up a meeting or something."

With a sigh, Jagger dipped his head at the priest.

The water was lukewarm—it felt good. When every bit of dust and sweat was removed, the bald priest handed him a clean, white kilt then led him to a cushy stool with golden, lion's paw feet. Another priest entered and laid platters of food on a small chest. Okay, it may be a prison, but at least it was a clean one, with food that smelled like Heaven on a plate. He was beyond famished and surprised he had any appetite at all.

"You said I could see my sister if I scrubbed off the grime." He glanced at the food, stomach rumbling. He ached to dig into the spread, but first he needed to make sure Aria was safe.

The large priest held up a finger then walked out.

A few seconds later, the door opened, and Aria rushed in. She was clean, dressed in a simple, white, linen shift. Her wet curls were pulled back into a fresh, fat braid. Her purple purse hung from her shoulder.

"Food," she squeaked when she saw him surrounded by a feast that rivaled the god's.

Jagger almost smiled. His sister's appetite was as mysterious to him as her mood swings. She actually enjoyed trying new things, often opting for sushi or tandoor even when burgers were an option. At the moment, Jagger was too hungry to care. He dug into the fruit, smelly white cheese, and aromatic stew with abandon.

Casting a glance at the nearby priest, Aria whispered with a mouthful of food. "Did they say anything about Herihor?"

"No," Jagger replied. "They didn't say anything at all. But we're here now. We'll just have to see what they do." He glanced at the priest, wondering if he sounded cooler than he felt, or if his sister saw right through him.

The truth was, Jagger usually felt superior to his sister. He was used to being the smart one, always annoyed by his needy, little sis. But he was grudgingly impressed by Aria's quick thinking since they got here. He felt a little intimidated. He wanted to prove he was up to this challenge. But what if he wasn't? Did Aria wonder too? She would soon, if she didn't already. Why on earth had the gods chosen him?

"Why do you look like someone just stole your A+ homework assignment?" she whispered.

Jagger sniffed a mystery-meat kabob. It smelled delightful, but his appetite died.

Aria considered him over pursed lips. "You know we're going to do this, right? It'll be fine."

He dropped his head back, sighing. "What exactly makes you so confident? Fighting with giant crocodiles? Having an asthma attack when you're stuck inside an ancient float, maybe?"

A red fruit was lifted for examination. She plopped it in her mouth and shrugged. "For a genius, you're really not that bright. We already succeeded. Don't you see?"

Jagger shook his head. What was she talking about now?

"The gemstones were in the tomb. On the *ankh*! If they were there in the future, that means we succeeded." She smiled, obviously proud of her powers of deduction.

Jagger moaned. "Wrong. Did you see them? They weren't real. They were like ghost stones. If you were right, real stones would have been there … if that's even how this stuff works."

Aria narrowed her eyes and bit her lips. "But … Why?"

"I don't know!" He stood up, and the piece of cheese resting on his knee dropped to the floor. "Maybe it was a hint from the gods, like Tatia said." Jagger fidgeted with the hem of his kilt—he couldn't believe this stuff was coming out of his mouth. "Or maybe they represented the possibility. You know, like it's *possible* Kevin Durant will suddenly appear, scoop us up, take us home, and give me a basketball contract."

"That's not possible—"

"Exactly!"

Creak.

The door shot open, and the old man they'd seen when they tumbled out of the float walked in. Without a word, the priest pulled up a nearby stool and eyed the siblings from head to toe. He crossed his arms and sat up straight.

"Much better." He nodded. "*This* is how one dresses to appear before the High Priest of Amun-Ra."

HOLY HERIHOR

"So you *are* Herihor?" Aria dropped the fig she was about to eat.

"I am." He leaned forward, dark eyes sparkling under gray-speckled eyebrows. He shifted his gaze to Jagger. "And you would be wise to remember that I am no fool, as if I would not recognize the true voice of a god I have served my entire life. Now, having agreed on who I am, let us discuss the two of you. How did you get the princess's amulet?"

The amulet! Jagger took it off when he cleaned himself. And worse, he'd set his phone down.

There! His sweat-drenched, old kilt, neatly folded, was on a stool near the stone basin. The priest standing next to it handed Jagger a small stack: phone, kilt, gold armbands, amulet. It was all there. Jagger nodded as he took it, shoving his phone in his new kilt's pocket, and stringing the amulet back around his neck.

"Tatia … I mean, Meretaten gave it to me," Jagger finally responded, looking Herihor directly in the eye. The High Priest reminded Jagger of his second-grade teacher, Mr. Norton, who was mean to every kid in class but Jagger. The teacher's-favorite-nerd treatment caused Jagger endless problems with the other kids. That was before the divorce, before homeschool, when things were normal.

The old priest leaned back on his stool, staring at them over folded arms. "Why? Why would Meretaten give you her most prized possession? Who are you two?"

The kids glanced at each other.

To tell the truth or think up another lie?

Jagger was sick of disguises. Besides, Tatia told them this was their guy—if they wanted the High Priest's help, they needed him to know the truth. Jagger exhaled, collecting his thoughts. The story erupted from his mouth like vomit. He left nothing out. He told him about Tatia's voice in his head, about seeing Mek, barely clinging to life. He told him about the Death Spell the General was planning to cast—a spell that would doom the royal family. He told him he and Aria were related to the royal family, that they'd die along with their very distant relatives if the spell was cast. He told him about Smenkare rescuing them and Mut's belief that the prince was working with the General. He told him of Mut's faith in Babi. When he got to the part about the crocodiles, Herihor eyed Aria's purse with curiosity. When the tale was done, the old man sat silently, rubbing his hands together like a villain in an old movie.

"That story is simply too strange to be untrue," he conceded. "You say the *Seshep ny Netjer* split in two before joining with you?" He shook his head. "Inexplicable, that is." Herihor considered Jagger with pursed lips. "I believe you," he announced.

Jagger bowed his head, relieved. Okay, step one accomplished. Now they just needed this guy to figure out what to do ... and help them do it.

"Only those of us who have had the pleasure of watching the princess speak to the gods would believe in her ability to cast the *Meseneh Rek* spell," Herihor said. "Remarkable magic, that is. Meretaten's abilities are ... unique. Now." He set a rolled papyrus scroll on the table. "I have something for you."

Jagger picked it up. Aria leaned closer as he unrolled it. "Our letter of introduction." Jagger scanned the cursive version of hieroglyphs. He couldn't read it—that talent hadn't magically been bestowed with their understanding of the language—but he recognized it instantly "How?" Jagger rubbed his stubbly head. He felt twitchy.

"You are the second pair of children to visit me this

morning," Herihor explained. "The others came through the front door." He glowered. "They said they were sent by Meretaten in order to gain my support in their efforts to thwart the General's plans to cast a powerful spell. It seemed preposterous. The *Heqa-oo Moot* has not been cast in generations—it is a terribly dangerous spell, and only the most accomplished magician could successfully cast it."

Jagger realized he was holding his breath. The General really did know about them. Some battle-thirsty, old General was looking for him and his little sister, hoping to erase them from existence.

"And did you give it to them? Your help?" Aria leaned forward, as if getting closer to the old priest would render him more willing to support them.

The High Priest's scowl deepened. "I have already explained that I am not easily fooled, young woman. Or should I say, princess?" His bushy brows crept up.

Aria flashed him one of her I'm-so-cute-you-can't-stay-annoyed-with-me smiles as she nodded her head.

Jagger thought Herihor was going to smile back, but he must be one of the rare people immune to Aria's charms. The High Priest shook his head and went on. "I called them liars and tossed them out. Now that I have heard your story, the incident makes more sense. The prince is, beyond question, the least talented person to be born into that family in generations, aside from Pharaoh, although that fact is for your ears only—I've long suspected Akhenaten's hatred of the old gods stems from his lack of ability." Herihor leaned forward. "Oh, Pharaoh and his unpopular son both know some magic. But frankly, I am surprised Smenkare managed to call Sobek's crocs. The idea that he is going to cast the *Heqa-oo Moot* is astounding, especially with the gods in decline. Only Thebes, and perhaps Memphis, is left with enough magic for such a spell, thanks largely to me and my priests. Clearly sending some local kids with a half-baked story was the prince's idea. The General, for all his flaws, is far too smart to think he can fool me so easily."

Jagger licked his lips. This was getting too real. "But you'll help us, right?" His voice cracked.

Herihor stood up. "I will do what I can." He rested his hands on the high back of an empty chair. "In truth, I am not sure how much I can do for you. I suppose we should start by figuring out where the gemstones are." The old man paused and stared down at Jagger.

Jagger squirmed.

"Helloooo." Aria folded her arms and cocked her head to the side. "You have a magic amulet now, Brainy."

Duh. Outsmarted by his sister again. *Great!* Wondering if time travel had shaved off IQ points, he clutched the Isis Knot in his palm, focusing on the gemstones. *There!* He could feel them, as well as Mut and her two companions, across the Nile. Babi was still close, he realized. "The gemstones are on the West Bank, past the Workman's Village."

The old man nodded to the nearby priest, and seconds later, a map was placed before them. It showed the West Bank of Thebes: the old palace complex, Malkata; the Valley of the Kings where the pharaohs were buried; and the Workmen's Village where Mut and her sidekicks were creating a diversion.

"Here." Jagger pointed at the cliffs where he felt the stones. "Smenkare is there too. I can feel him."

"Of course." The High Priest nodded. "They are in one of the kings' tombs. That is the Valley of the Kings, where the pharaohs lie. The gemstones will be safe there until the spell is cast. They will select a family tomb. It will make Meketaten's *Ka* even more powerful if an ancestor is near. Is the General with them?"

"I don't know. I've never met him, so I can't tell—"

Whack!

The door flew open.

Jagger jumped to his feet and stepped in front of Aria. Two unfamiliar priests shoved another priest into the room. He fell at their feet while the two priests who brought him stood by the door, looking bruised and battered. And angry.

"Don't touch me!" The guy on the floor looked up.

"Babi!" Aria ran to him.

Now dressed as a priest, newly shaven head and all, the captain had a black eye and scratches down his chest. The two guys who'd captured him looked even worse.

"You're safe." He jumped up, and brushed himself off, sending a vicious glance at the other priests.

"The brave captain I presume?" Herihor lifted a fuzzy, gray brow. "Trusted intimate of the noble Mutbenret and the princess Meretaten?"

Babi nodded, examining Jagger and Aria like they were goods bound for his hull.

"Sit." Herihor motioned to a nearby stool. "You seem to be making a habit of attempting to thwart my security to sneak into Amun-Ra's temple. An unbeliever, I presume. For no one who believed in the gods would dare enter the sacred sanctuary so brazenly. And twice in one day."

Babi flashed a tired smile. "On the contrary, I simply believe the gods have more important things to worry about than silly rules, like who can and can't enter their homes. Things like ensuring the success of these two kids, for example."

Herihor nodded, conceding the point.

The captain looked at Jagger with a raised brow.

"We told him everything," Jagger admitted. "He says he'll help us."

"I said I would try," Herihor clarified.

"I presume the kids spotted leaving the temple earlier had Meretaten's letter of introduction?" Babi glanced at the High Priest.

"Clever deduction." Herihor nodded. "And accurate."

"The kids are in the Valley of the Kings now," the captain continued.

Herihor's eyes widened. "That makes sense. The gemstones are there too. And the prince is with them, in one of the family tombs." Herihor's fluffy brows drew together. "But which one, and how you will get there unseen and retrieve them, I do not yet know."

"Amenhotep the Second's tomb," Babi said.

Herihor's brows crawled higher.

"The two kids were followed," Babi explained. "But there's no way to approach the tomb unseen. Hopefully the General and Smenkare believe Jagger and Aria are in the Workmen's Village with Mut. No one has gone in or out of the Village since she and her two barrels went in."

"Hmmm." Herihor nodded. "That tomb makes the approach a little easier." He looked at Jagger and Aria, explaining, "The Valley is shaped like a crescent. Amenhotep the Second's tomb is on the back, left quadrant." The High Priest pointed to a location on the map. Clutching the amulet tight, Jagger confirmed the gemstones were there. "I can get you there," Herihor continued. "The problem will be getting the gemstones and getting out without being captured."

"You think?" Aria whispered.

The High Priest opened a cedar chest and retrieved a papyrus scroll and a long, wooden box. Jagger recognized the traditional scribal equipment: several holes filled with black and red pigment and a few reeds for writing. Quickly, Herihor mapped out the tomb. A long hall led downward, punctuated by steps, until reaching a larger antechamber supported by two pillars. A final staircase led off to the left into the main burial chamber, supported by six pillars with four small storerooms adjoining, two on each side.

"Great." Aria rolled her eyes. "Another tomb!"

Jagger wracked his brain for ideas, wondering if they could tunnel in, or if there was some kind of hidden door they could sneak in and out of. "Any chance there's a way in that doesn't include going through the front door?"

Herihor chuckled, deep in his throat, shaking his head as he stretched. "The pharaohs have gone to great lengths to ensure their tombs are secure from intruders."

Babi leaned back on his stool, rubbing his newly bald head as he studied the map.

Taking his phone from his kilt pocket, Jagger snapped a picture of the tomb layout, thinking it might come in handy. The phone camera flashed in the dim light of the room.

"Ah!" Herihor stepped back. The priest standing guard at the far end of the room squealed. "What is it?" The old priest pointed at the phone as if it were a creature of chaos.

Jagger smiled as he flipped through his pictures, selecting the tomb shot and showing his screen to the old priest.

Herihor's eyes flew open wide. "What magic ..." He shook his head.

Jagger knew it was petty, but it made him feel good. He was out of his element here, just a nerdy kid suddenly running around with princesses and magicians and High Priests. It was intimidating to be the runt of the litter all the time. Even his little sister was outperforming him, fitting in like she was born in ancient Egypt, even though, unlike Jagger, she knew nothing about the country's history.

"We'll just have to be prepared to deal with whatever we encounter." Babi's voice reclaimed Jagger's attention. "It won't be the first time I've gone into a battle with no plan."

Aria stared at him, legs crossed and sandaled toe bouncing. "And do you usually win?"

Babi smiled. "I'm still here aren't I?"

"And this time, you'll have a magician along as well," Herihor added, smiling back at the captain.

SNAKE HASTE

Jagger wiped sleep from his eyes as Herihor led the three of them through twisting, temple hallways, a few hours before dawn. They were sneaking out the temple's back door, like thieves in the night, in case the General had the temple under surveillance.

Light from the old priest's torch cast eerie shadows against the beige, stone walls. Aria stomped along in front of Jagger, who reviewed Herihor and Babi's plan over and over in his head. At least someone *had* a plan. Jagger knew *he* was no match for an ancient General and his magical sidekick, even if Smenkare really was magically challenged. What was Jagger going to do? Read to them while Aria flashed her cute smile?

His nerves buzzed as he followed the priest through twists

and turns until they came to a dead end. "What ..." Jagger banged a hand against the wall, then shook it—that hurt.

"Patience." Herihor's voice was stern. Handing the torch to Babi, the High Priest faced the blank, stone wall. His hands traced shapes in the air as he mumbled.

With a zap, the stone turned to mist. One second the wall was impenetrable. The next, it was a cloud of cool steam. A burst of red twinkled in the dim light, fading as Herihor led them through the mist and out into the dark night.

The fresh air felt good against Jagger's skin. He scanned the small, outdoor shrine, then stared back at the wall, which stood in the space he'd just walked through. He pushed his hand against it. Rock solid.

"We just walked right through that wall." Aria sighed, eyes wide.

"Come." Herihor pointed the way. Babi waved Jagger and Aria on, taking up a position in the rear as he peered around columns that peppered the shrine, which was built behind the temple's soaring, back wall.

Jagger's stomach churned. To the right, he could see the edges of the sacred lake, glimmering in the moonlight. The temple wall was inscribed with colorful images of the gods. They looked alert, as if the starlight animated them.

Crunch!

"Sorry!" Aria's hand flew to her mouth. She stared down at her sandal before leaning over to pick up two small pieces of pottery. Holding them together, she crinkled her forehead. "It's an ear!"

Jagger took the pieces from her hand and tossed them, grabbed her arm, and dragged her on. Babi looked tense behind them, now dressed as a sailor again, but bald, and with more weapons than any sailor would have carted around.

"It's a religious thing." Jagger kept his voice low. "Regular folks, who didn't have the clout to get inside the temple, could talk to the gods from outside the temple. Some people would donate clay ears … you know, to make sure they were heard."

"Because they didn't think their gods had their own ears?"

Jagger rolled his eyes. His sister had no appreciation for historical artifacts. He pushed Aria toward the High Priest, who led them away from the sacred lake. They flanked the long, high wall of the temple, weaving through columns and past inscriptions, any one of which, once translated, would wow the socks off any ivy towered dissertation committee.

Jagger craned his neck back to see the tops of the columns. The scale of the temple was astounding. It wasn't easy to impress a well-traveled kid from Chicago with big buildings, but this one definitely did the trick. And he'd thought the ruins that still existed in his time were impressive. The real thing was a stunner.

Aria shifted closer to him as they spilled out of the temple complex. The Nile was just ahead. Jagger assumed Herihor was leading them to the quay, jutting into the river, and was surprised when the priest made a sharp right turn and headed into a nearby series of buildings that reeked of animals and, worse, animal waste. With all the creatures slaughtered in the temple, it made sense to keep them close. The smell also explained why they burned so much incense.

"Wait here," Herihor ordered. He disappeared behind a high, stone gate, returning moments later with four donkeys. With a quick nod, he led them back to the quay and whistled once, quietly. Two silent men in white kilts rowed up a flat boat, and they all, donkeys included, boarded the boat and crossed to the west bank.

Herihor climbed gracefully onto a donkey as soon as they jumped off the boat. "Let's go."

"On that?" Jagger pointed at the donkey, who shifted so its butt was in Jagger's face.

"What? You don't have donkeys in the future?" Jagger couldn't tell if Babi's question was sincere or sarcastic.

"Tell us nothing of your future," the High Priest intoned before Jagger could respond. "Meretaten is messing with powerful forces, bringing you two back. It is essential you keep the future out of the past." Herihor turned his donkey around and, somehow, made the beast jog into the night.

"You're a pretty girl." Aria stared into her donkey's eyes, petting its ears.

"Boy," Babi corrected her.

She shrugged. With a boost from the captain, she

scrambled onto Dino—because yes, his sister had named the beast—then followed the priest.

"Keep the future out of the past," Jagger mumbled as he pulled himself clumsily onto his donkey's back. It took three tries, but he finally got up ... without the help of Babi, who loitered, watching him with a bemused grin. "I'm fine," Jagger insisted, right before his donkey turned the wrong way.

"Come on, girl." Babi caught Jagger's donkey and led her toward Aria and Herihor. Jagger rolled his eyes and concentrated on not falling off.

The ride was torture. An hour later, Jagger's butt was sore, and sweat streamed down every part of his body. The heat increased by the minute—it was like the air itself was on fire. On the bright side, he and his donkey had made a truce—she walked placidly, and he rubbed her behind the ears every ten minutes or so, thanking her for the ride.

Aria had, predictably, risen to the occasion. She flashed Jagger a smile as they trotted along. How could she smile knowing they were headed toward almost certain death, in temperatures that would make Satan himself uncomfortable, on beasts that probably wanted to eat their toes for dinner?

"Your inhaler," he began as his donkey shifted next to hers.

"I'm fine," she insisted. "You worry about you. And Sasha."

Jagger squeezed Sasha's reins tighter. "I could have at least named my own donkey," he sulked, annoyed by his sister's levity. Jagger's molecules were humming. It was as if his DNA could feel the doom riding to meet them. The closer they got, the sicker he felt. The idea of rescuing the gemstones, and the princess, and his own family, was beyond absurd. What was he going to do when they got there? Getting into the tomb was one thing. Getting out with the gemstones, alive, seemed impossible.

He hated feeling so dependent on Herihor and, worse, Babi. He wished Tatia was here. Or at least Mut. What kind of Protector left them with a random ship captain as soon as things got tough? He glanced back at Babi, who winked annoyingly.

Jagger grimaced. Mom would murder him if she knew he was letting Aria ride into danger … on an ancient Egyptian donkey … named Dino!

After riding north, skimming the river, they'd turned west toward towering, red cliffs. Now, they were well up into the cliffs behind the Valley of the Kings, where Amenhotep and other Eighteenth Dynasty pharaohs were laid to rest. Pink sand filled the landscape everywhere Jagger looked as they rode higher and higher. He kept glancing at his sister, worried the heat would trigger her asthma.

Finally, Herihor stopped and climbed gracefully down from his donkey. Aria and Babi dismounted, and Jagger half fell, half climbed off Sasha, then rubbed his painful arms and legs and tried to stretch. He'd give his favorite high tops for a small breeze.

"We are here." Herihor drew a half circle in the sand, placing them behind the arch, just above where twelve o'clock would be if it were a clock. "Amenhotep's tomb is here." He drew a small "x" at the ten o'clock spot. "We'll come in right above the tomb, at the top of the cliff." He'd led them around the Theban peak so they could approach the tomb from the mountain, rather than through the valley where they'd be easily seen. "It's about a mile from here. We walk the rest of the way. You can't trust these creatures to stay quiet. They bray at the worst possible moments."

"But …" Jagger's mouth was as dry and parched as his imagination. "We …"

"Are the priests and sailors at the Workman's Village?" Babi asked.

Jagger clutched the amulet and nodded. "With Mut."

"Good." Babi had advised creating a ruckus at the Village to draw the General and Smenkare's attention away from the tomb. Herihor sent a bunch of priests out, along with some townspeople, on some trumped-up pretense. A few of Babi's sailors tagged along.

"But isn't the Village supposed to be empty now?" Jagger knew the Village traditionally housed hundreds of skilled artisans, the workmen who built the pharaohs' tombs. But when Akhenaten moved the capital to Amarna, the people who lived there should have gone too.

"Not entirely." Babi shrugged. "Some people stayed put.

There's an old *medji* policeman there who refused to move. He's fond of Mut." The captain's eyes twinkled—clearly he shared the sentiment. "He'll let her stay as long as she likes. She's delightful, after all, and Hemet and Mutef are useful to have around."

"But what if ..." Jagger shook his head. "What if your idea didn't work? The General might still be in the tomb." His heart hammered against his chest. Jagger didn't really buy the ruse idea, but he'd kept his mouth shut. It's not like he had a better plan. Being annihilated along with half of his family wasn't a great fallback option.

"Where's Smell-kare?" Aria asked.

Jagger wrapped a sweaty palm around the amulet again. "Near the Village," he acknowledged. "The gemstones are still in the tomb. But I don't know where the General is. He might be there, waiting for us, snacking on crackers and sharpening a long knife." He wiped sweat off his stubbly head. The sun was now high in a bright, blue sky, drenching them in its heat.

"We'll know soon enough." Babi shared a tight grin.

"Let's go." Herihor kicked up red dust as he twirled away and started climbing the slope.

"Wait!" It took Jagger a second to realize the word came out of his own mouth. "Uh, I mean, now? Shouldn't we make a plan or something? What about that long, sharp knife?" He knew he should make an effort to hide his fear, but, like the quest to get the stones, it seemed hopeless.

Aria patted his back like he was her puppy. "We'll just have to do our best."

How could she act so calm? Jagger knew, deep down, that his greatest fear wasn't dying. Death would just be the same oblivion he had, or rather hadn't, experienced before he was born. It wasn't even that their family would cease to exist. He'd be dead too, so he'd be oblivious if that happened. His true fear was that he'd fail Mom. And Aria. The worst-case scenario was surviving and returning to Mom, and Grams and Gramps, without his sister.

"We don't have a choice, remember?" Aria pulled his mind back to the moment. "If we don't at least try, we're both gonna die, probably along with Mom and Grams, or maybe Gramps, and the princess, and a bunch of other people who are family, even if we don't know them. And poor Mek will be extra dead. What could happen to us that would be worse than that? Besides, you'll come up with something when you need to. Who knows? Maybe gum will save the day again."

"We're out of gum," Jagger grumbled.

Her pep talk had done nothing to dispel the gloomy feeling that weighed him down, but he was too smart not to acknowledge the flawless logic. Jagger nodded to the priest to lead them on.

The effort to merely breathe as they scaled the Theban peak—the high point of the cliffs behind the Valley of the Kings that looked like a natural pyramid—soon required all his attention. Aria stopped to suck from her asthma inhaler, pulling a small spray bottle out of her purse. She sprayed herself, then looked to Jagger, her eyebrows leapt up to question him, as if to say, *hey want some of my perfume ... because that really matters right now!*

Jagger shook his head. What on earth she was thinking?

She shrugged and sprayed him anyway. He flinched as water, with a hint of mint, cooled him. She smiled and turned to catch up with Herihor.

"She's resourceful." The captain grinned and waved Jagger on.

Aria stopped suddenly, and Jagger bumped into her. "Who's *he* talking to?" she asked.

Herihor was at the top of the peak, waving his arms, talking animatedly.

"Go." The captain put a hand on Aria, pushing her forward for a better view.

Jagger gasped when he saw a gargantuan cobra, facing the old priest.

Jagger froze in his tracks. How many over-sized reptiles were they going to run into? This one wasn't as humongous as the crocs or Apep, but it certainly wasn't a run-of-the-mill snake. It was black with copper spots; red eyes pierced its flat, wide head.

"So pretty," Aria breathed.

His sister was right. It was beautiful, in its own scaly way.

It was also angry … if snakes could get angry. It seemed to be arguing with the priest, hissing and sticking out its tongue. The priest talked back, too quietly for Jagger to hear.

"Stay silent," Babi hissed as he cast his eyes down, grabbing a kid in each hand. "She likes silence."

"Who?" Aria whispered back. "Who's *she*?"

"Meretseger?" Jagger breathed the question. Could this snake actually be the goddess of the Theban peak? The goddess whose name meant "she who loves silence?" Was he supposed to believe this was the actual goddess? Or was it like the crocs, sent by some magician? And if so, who sent her? Smenkare? Did that mean he knew they were coming?

Books really didn't explain this stuff well—a disturbing, and new, thought.

The snake reared back. And spit.

The world slowed down as the spittle hurtled toward the priest's head.

Herihor must have known it was coming. He held up a hand, and the spit dissolved, turning to mist like the temple wall had hours earlier. Red lights twinkled above his head.

"Smells sour," Aria mumbled.

The snake hissed. Then spun and slithered away, shrinking into a regular, old snake as she slid into a nearby hole.

Jagger shook his head, wondering if he'd imagined the whole thing. Maybe the heat was getting to him. Or the stress.

"Come." The High Priest waved them forward.

Babi's fingers tightened on Jagger's arm. He looked stunned, eyeing the old man warily.

Jagger sighed. He had no idea what that strange episode meant, but his sister was right: moving forward was their only option. He hung his head and led his sister toward danger.

SEIZE THE ... SPRAY?

They stared down the cliff wall into the valley from their perch just above Amenhotep's tomb. Jagger's legs felt like jelly. He wondered if the others could hear his knees knocking together.

Aria slid her hand into his. He cringed, embarrassed she felt the need to comfort him. He glanced over at her: she was white as a sheet. She wasn't doing it for him. She was doing it for her. If Aria was terrified, things were past bad.

"We're okay." His voice was two octaves too high.

"Breathe," she whispered.

This was it. They might not see the light of day again. But a whole lot of people were relying on him to do his part. And if Tatia was correct, he had no choice.

"You were right. We have to try." He squeezed her hand, and she flashed him her I'm-pretending-this-is-okay grin—the grin she usually reserved for their passing interactions with Dad.

"Let's go." Babi tied a rope to a rock so they could drop to the valley floor. "Two guards. Over there." He pointed.

"I'll handle them." Herihor crouched at the cliff's edge, hands raised. "Are you ready?"

At Babi's nod, the High Priest whispered into the wind, whipping his hands back and forth. Jagger couldn't make out the words, but a stiff breeze kicked up immediately, blowing sand into the valley and creating a wall of dust in front of the cliff. Red lights glimmered as the sand rose higher, hiding them from the guards' view. It looked natural, wafting left and right, then up and down.

"Quickly. It won't last long." Herihor lowered himself onto the rope.

Jagger wasn't much of an athlete, and the private school he'd attended before the divorce hadn't exactly taught rope scaling, but the old man got down it easily enough, and Babi motioned for Jagger to go next. The rope burned his palms as he eased himself down, using his legs to balance against the cliff wall, finding footholds where he could. It took him longer than Herihor, but he got to the ground in one piece, and his sister was just behind him.

Babi landed last, and the old man nodded to a nearby hole in the cliff wall.

The tomb.

Should it be open? It might as well have *TRAP* written in flashing lights above it.

Jagger swallowed the bile that crawled up his throat. Taking a deep breath, he steeled himself to follow the priest in before realizing Aria wasn't behind him. He twirled in place, panicked. She was next to the cliff wall, playing with the rope.

"What are you doing?" Jagger hissed.

"Hiding it," she replied. "There." She stepped back to view her work. Jagger had to admit, it was good thinking. The rope that had been just hanging there, announcing to anyone who looked this way that someone had just dropped from the cliff above, was now tucked neatly into a crack in the wall, secured by a hair scrunchy from Aria's purse.

She blew out a puff of air, then gave Jagger a quick nod. This was it.

"Let's go." Herihor waved them toward their fate. He paused just inside the tomb to let their eyes adjust. It was dim. And it would get darker as they went deeper.

Jagger grabbed his phone and flipped on its flashlight.

Herihor gasped. He stared, open mouthed, at the illumination bouncing off the tomb walls, then he nodded approvingly. Modern day America may not have magic, but it did have some pretty cool tech.

Jagger cast his light down the top few stairs. They couldn't see far. After listening for a moment, hearing nothing but their own breath, Herihor led them forward. Jagger pushed Aria in front of him, where he could see her, and folded himself between her and Babi, who brought up the rear.

The priest led them into a narrow corridor that slanted downward. Jagger's heart raced as he walked into the abyss—an abyss he might never emerge from. He stayed close to Aria as they followed another staircase downward, then another descending corridor that opened into a small, square room. A deep pit covered the floor.

"It's a well," Jagger mumbled, watching Herihor skirt it.

Jagger shifted in front of his sister. He hugged the wall, balancing on the narrow space that circled the hole.

Aria paused at the edge, biting her lip. "What's it for?" she whispered.

Jagger stopped and looked back at her. "Maybe for floodwaters. Or to fool tomb robbers. Or maybe it's part of their religion—like the waters of creation to help Pharaoh's rebirth." He swallowed hard. "Doesn't matter. It's just a hole. We can get past it."

"I know," she peeped as she began creeping around the edge.

When Jagger turned back, Herihor had reached the other side of the well and disappeared through a doorway. Jagger caught up, peeking into the small room that was painted to look like a giant papyrus roll covered in hieroglyphs: beige and black, with accents of red and yellow. The stale smell was overwhelming.

"AAAHHHH!"

Jagger whipped around, heart in his throat. "Aria!"

She was frozen in place, balanced in the narrow space between the hole and the wall, eyes glued to something in the pit.

"Scorpion," Jagger breathed.

That was a colossal understatement. The thing was enormous. It clung to the side of the well. It was six feet long from its head to the end of its long tail, and its pincers were about two feet each. It slashed at Aria. Its tail slapped the far wall, lashing out to sting. Mist drifted around the oversized creature, filling the hole so Jagger couldn't see the bottom. Were there more monsters behind this one?

"Run." Jagger urged his sister toward him, moving to the side so she could run into the pillared room ahead of him.

Zap!

A familiar hissing sound: the door filled with mist and sand. Jagger threw his body against it. Blocked. The back door was similarly filled. Babi shoved against the mist, then turned and shook his head. They were trapped in this room with the creature.

"Herihor!" Jagger shouted.

He heard the High Priest chanting on the other side of the blocked door. Jagger couldn't make out the words. Herihor must be trying to get to them.

"Help us," Jagger yelled.

"One moment. I need to undo this spell."

Jagger looked back at his sister. Aria threw her body from side to side, weaving to avoid the giant pincers as she struggled not to lose her balance.

Arrows bounced off the walls. Babi was searching for the creature's weak spot, but the arrows ricocheted off its natural armor, useless.

Jagger couldn't move. His worst fear was here. Aria was going to die, and he would just stand here and watch it all, too scared to budge.

"Almost there," Herihor yelled.

Almost wasn't good enough.

"No!" Jagger's primal scream bounced around the small room. It was as if a hidden compartment in his gut opened up, barfing out anger Jagger didn't even realize he'd buried deep. Anger at Dad for being unavailable and irresponsible. Anger at Mom for leaving him in charge all the time, making it impossible to just be a kid. Even anger at Grams and Gramps for being old; the truth was, Jagger took care of them more than they took care of him. And anger at Aria for needing him so much. Jagger watched after himself by the time he was eleven. Why couldn't she?

But along with the bile came a realization: he didn't want to protect his sister because it was his duty. She was the only other person on the planet who shared his bizarre life, who understood what it was like to bounce back and forth between Mom and Grams and Gramps and, on occasion, Dad, not to mention whatever continent they landed on.

All that occurred to him in an instant, and he knew he needed to do something. If he didn't act, he'd never forgive himself. An old Martin Luther King Jr. quote thundered through his head: *If a man has not discovered something that he will die for, he isn't fit to live.*

Aria was worth dying for.

Jagger tensed, ready to throw his body onto the scorpion, driving them both into the pit to their deaths, sacrificing himself to save his little sis.

Okay, so that was Plan B.

First, he needed to get to his sister.

Move!

Sliding around the narrow space, he eased himself over to Aria. She looked terrified, eyes bright and skin sallow. She was staring intensely at the big bug, trying to read its intentions so she could dodge the next pincer move.

More arrows bounced off the walls, and Babi cursed, dropping his bow and pulling out a sword. Moving to the far side of the well, he screamed at the scorpion. He banged the sword against the rock, trying to pull the creature's attention away from Aria.

"Face me, you ugly beast," he yelled.

It worked.

The scorpion scurried to the other side, toward Babi, just

as Jagger reached Aria. Grabbing her hand, he pulled her forward and shoved her against the sand-filled doorway, but their path was still blocked.

"Now, Herihor!" Jagger yelled as he put himself between Aria and the creature.

"I am trying," the priest shot back. "I am occupied fighting my own battle at the moment. Just hang on." The old man sounded winded. Jagger wondered what kind of monster he was facing.

What if what was on the other side of this door was even worse than the scorpion? At least Jagger was now between his sister and imminent death—that was something.

Aria grit her teeth and scowled. "We have to do something. We have to pull it together and do something. We can't fail Mek," she wailed, as if the princess was here battling a giant scorpion, rather than them.

Jagger's brain ticked through possibilities, scanning the small room for anything they could use, rubbing his hands down his own body as if he might find a giant bug-repelling machine gun hanging at his side.

"Your purse. Anything in your purse we can use?"

Aria shook her head, then paused, bright eyes looking at Jagger in surprise. "Maybe." She rummaged through it and pulled out a small spray can. Jagger wasn't sure what she thought minty water was going to do for them.

"Babi," she yelled. "Catch." She threw the can, and the

captain caught it. Slashing at the creature with the sword, now in his left hand, he grasped the can with his right.

"Spray it at him. Try to get his face, his ... eye thingy."

"What's water going to do to a giant scorpion?" Jagger prayed the mist would drop so Herihor could magic the creature away, like Mut had the crocodiles.

"It's not water."

Babi sprayed the scorpion in the face.

The creature paused, as if stunned for a moment.

"Keep spraying," Aria yelled.

Babi leaned toward the creature, aimed the canister at its eyes, and pumped over and over.

Jagger didn't know if normal scorpions could screech, but this one did. The racket ricocheted off the walls as it screamed, falling into the well on its back. Steam erupted from the hole, covering them all in a damp mist. The scream echoed around the chamber for a moment longer.

Thunk.

Hiss.

Then silence.

Babi and Jagger stared at Aria. The sound of Jagger's heart was loud in his ears.

"What was that?" Jagger looked down at the menacing hole. Steam wafted out from it but dissipated before reaching them.

"Bug spray." Aria massaged her head with her hands.

"From the girl's weekend camping trip Mom and I took last summer."

Jagger remembered the weekend. He'd spent a rare Saturday night alone with Dad while they were gone. He'd been looking forward to it and remembered how secretly relieved he was that it actually happened, and that Dad had been in a good mood. Dad had even played violent video games with him—games Mom would never let him play.

Zap.

The sand blocking the door to the next chamber fell to the ground in a heap.

Jagger and Aria stumbled forward, Babi on their heels.

"Thank the gods, you're safe." Herihor waved them to the left, toward the stairs that led down into the large, tomb chamber.

Jagger grabbed Aria's hand and pulled her toward it.

Two steps later, something hard struck his head.

Blackness took him.

THAT'S THE GENERAL IDEA

Jagger moaned. His head was pounding. He opened his eyes—it hurt. He rolled over, squinting to adjust to the dim light. The lump next to him was Aria, lying on her back with her eyes open.

"Aria!" His hand shot out to touch her. She was warm. And breathing. He exhaled.

She blinked, and tears gathered in her eyes. She struggled to sit up, holding her head with both arms and groaning. "Where are we?"

Jagger turned his thumping head. They were in a small, dank room, carved out of rough stone. Babi was lying next to them, out cold. "Where's Herihor?" Jagger mumbled. He grabbed his amulet: the High Priest was close. A jab of hope rushed through him. Maybe he was working on their rescue plan right now.

"Babi." Aria rolled over and poked the captain. "Wake up."

The captain's eyes fluttered. He opened them and growled, then felt around for his weapons. They were gone. "What happened?" Babi's eyes moved past Jagger and froze.

Following the captain's stare, Jagger saw another sand filled door. Long, vertical bars of mist and sand stretched from floor to ceiling. It offered a view into the burial chamber beyond. They must be in one of the small, storage rooms adjoining it.

Scooting to the door, Jagger looked out at beautifully decorated walls covered in more papyrus scroll décor. The room was illuminated by flames from torches, which were stuck to the walls every few feet. The ceiling was painted dark blue, peppered with thousands of stars. A large, red quartzite sarcophagus was just in front of them, at the bottom of a short flight of stairs. Wide columns filled the space, covered with images of the gods.

A voice leaked out from the next chamber, and Jagger stilled, straining to hear.

"If you had done your job right in the first place, they would not be here at all."

He knew that voice.

He clutched the amulet, heart pounding.

Herihor!

"Yes, unlike my crocodiles, your scorpion really finished them off," a familiar gravelly voice responded, dripping with sarcasm as Herihor entered the tomb chamber, the teenage prince grumbling behind him.

"With Smenkare," Babi breathed. "The priest was working with them all along. That's why the goddess ..." The captain paused, and dropped his head in his hands.

Jagger met Aria's eyes. She might not have his math skills, but she was obviously doing the same calculation he was: two magicians on the bad guys' side, none on theirs. Where was Mut when they needed her? Some Protector she'd turned out to be!

"Okay," Aria sighed. "So maybe *that* one we shouldn't have trusted."

"You think? How about both of them! You thought Smenkare was the Protector!" Jagger hissed. He fell onto his back, covering his face with his arms. Why had he trusted the High Priest so quickly? He had a rule never to trust people until they proved to be trustworthy. He'd been so desperate to get Herihor's help, he'd believed him simply because he wanted a powerful ally to save the day, mostly because he didn't think he could do it himself.

"Enough!" The new voice was deep and scratchy.

Jagger sat back up, craning his neck to see who was speaking.

"That's the General," Babi whispered.

All three men walked into view and stood in front of the sarcophagus: the prince, the High Priest, and another man, larger than either of them, with short, black hair, bulging muscles, and an immaculate, white kilt. His gold earring shimmered in the torchlight, and gold armbands circled his impressive biceps. The General was even scarier in real life than he'd been in Jagger's imagination.

"Forget about them," the General sneered. "We'll kill them before we leave. We needed you here, Herihor, and finally, here you are. If nothing else, these intruders managed to get you out of that temple. Now, start the *Heqa-oo Moot*! It's time to get this done."

"I told you, *I* can do it." Smenkare's voice cracked. "You didn't need to involve him. And you should have asked my permission before you did."

Herihor's bushy, gray eyebrows jumped in scorn. "Let us leave this one to the real magicians. The Death Spell is far beyond your abilities, boy." At least Herihor hadn't lied about his low opinion of the prince.

Smenkare turned away, probably to hide the blush creeping up his torso and neck.

Babi shoved Jagger sideways as the prince wandered their way. "Sleep," he whispered.

Jagger peeked through closed lids as the prince stared down at them through the bars. Smenkare walked off, scuffing his feet like a sulky teenager, kicking something in front of the door: Aria's purse, Jagger's phone, and Babi's sword.

"I think I can …" Aria lay on her stomach and reached her arm through the bars of mist. She squirmed, but she couldn't reach their stuff. She moaned and rolled back over, blinking away tears.

Jagger had never seen his sister look so dejected. Mad, often. Sad, sometimes. Dejected, never. He knew he should do something to help, but what could he say? Hard to put a positive spin on dying in an ancient tomb jail, knowing all the people that are relying on you were going to die too.

"Why?" Jagger turned to Babi.

"Oh, Brainy," Aria moaned. "You and your whys. Why does it matter why?"

"Because I don't understand. Why is Herihor helping them? Maybe if we knew why …"

The captain rubbed his bald head. "Who knows what drives people to do the things they do? Maybe Herihor wants to get rid of the family that supports Amun-Ra's rival god, the Aten. I'm no magician, but my understanding is that as the Aten's power grows, the magical abilities of the old gods' followers diminish. Herihor has had powers far too long to give them up easily."

"That doesn't make sense." Jagger shook his head. "By siding with the General, he's helping the Aten."

"Short term, perhaps. But if he gets rid of the royal

160

family, the Aten's power may fade away." Babi shrugged. "Or maybe he thinks the old gods are doomed, so he's switching sides. Maybe he believes the Aten will enhance his power. Or he just wants riches. Or maybe he's old and confused. I don't know. Blasted priest! I should have known not to trust a priest."

"*Ee-ee ti en ee,*" the old man started chanting, arms weaving madly. "Come to me."

Herihor held an alabaster, boomerang-shaped wand in the air. It was inscribed with scorpions, snakes, and frogs. Were the creatures wriggling? Jagger cringed. He never wanted to see another scorpion as long as he lived, but the squirming creatures didn't seem to bother Herihor. He placed one end of the wand on the ground and began to draw a shape on the floor. It was a triangle. The sarcophagus was at the flat end, inside the triangle's border. Smenkare and the General were inside as well. As the priest connected the final ends of the triangle, Jagger felt wind on his clammy skin and wondered briefly how there could be wind in the tomb, as if that was the oddest thing happening at the moment. Red tinted lights floated above the sarcophagus, spreading across the star-speckled ceiling.

Herihor pulled a green tinged scroll from his robes and stood at the point of the triangle, across from the sarcophagus. He motioned the prince and General to take up positions at the points to each side of the sarcophagus so that all three points of the triangle were occupied. "Come, mighty Aten."

The wind picked up. The eerie, red lights pulsed, and a sour smell surged through the chamber. A strong breeze whipped the lights around, loud in the silence of the tomb.

Jagger's gut clenched as he watched the old priest produce squares of wax and begin crafting what looked like small bodies.

"You depict the enemy of Aten. You are a threat to our country. Your name will be written. You will be spat on, trodden on, and destroyed in the fire of the god." Herihor chanted this repeatedly, addressing each wax figure as his speedy hands fashioned them.

"Seven … eight … nine," Babi counted softly, and slowly, as the priest chanted, the wind whipping faster through the tomb. "There are nine. One for each of them: the king, the queen, their five daughters, the queen mother Tiye, and Tutankhamun. Smenkare gets left out, I'm guessing."

"Nine stones," Jagger mused. The number nine was powerful in ancient Egypt. The gods were usually organized in groups of three—a father, mother, and child. The Ennead was made up of nine gods. Potent stuff. He hadn't realized the family had nine members too, excluding Smenkare, of course. "Tatia said there'd be nine."

Jagger shook his head. It didn't make sense. Tatia had been certain every member of the royal family would die if this spell was cast. Did Smenkare know that? Could the princess have been wrong? If so, maybe their family would survive after all. They could be distant descendants of the corrupt prince. Jagger didn't love that idea—it did nothing to help Mek or the royal family—but it was better than the alternative.

Herihor scrawled on each wax figure with a reed pen, his deep voice chanting melodically as the red lights danced with the lights of the torches, animated by the wind. Jagger couldn't see what was written, but somehow he knew the old man was writing the names of the family members on the wax figurines. The prince and General watched in silence. Smenkare shifted his weight back and forth, bouncing on the balls of his feet.

"The nine are assembled, the Ennead is created," Herihor intoned. "The *Ka* will be shared, the *Ka* will be destroyed, the enemies of Aten will cease to be." He walked to the sarcophagus and placed the nine wax figures on top, holding his hand out to the prince.

Smenkare glared at the High Priest. Jagger thought the prince would refuse to cooperate.

"Now!" the General's nasally voice rang out.

The prince flinched, then handed Herihor a fine, linen bag. The old priest poured the stones onto the sarcophagus. Lifting the largest, green and rough, he examined it with a frightful smile. The wind whipped faster as if it recognized the stones, like a maelstrom was forming just outside the barred door.

"The *Ka*." The old man stuck the large, green stone into the largest wax figure and set it in the middle of the sarcophagus. Red lights erupted from the stone, sparks flying. "I name you Meketaten, daughter of the king's body, beloved of the queen …" The titles continued.

SSSssssssssss.

Jagger jumped as something close to them hissed.

HISSSSSY FIT

SSSSSSSsssssssssssssss.

The snake from the peak was just outside their cell, larger, shinier, and more majestic than any snake had a right to be.

"Meretseger." Babi dropped his head to the ground.

Aria grabbed Jagger's arm. She stared at the snake, biting her lip, as it slithered back and forth on the other side of the misty bars.

The old priest kept chanting. The snake's hissing, loud as it was, was drowned out by the roar of the wind.

"What does she want?" Aria whispered to Babi.

"I have no idea." The captain shook his head. "I've heard tales of the gods appearing to Pharaoh, or members of the royal family. I didn't believe them. Magicians claim to get their powers from the old gods, but few people have ever seen magic, outside of the healing magic practiced by the priests. I've only seen it a few times, which is more than most. Of course, most don't know Mut."

SSSSsssssss. The snake slithered left, then right.

Babi stared down at Meretseger intently, eyes gleaming. "Even a lowly ship's captain like me recognizes a goddess when she appears." He rubbed his knuckles. "She looked angry earlier. I don't think she's a fan of Herihor. Maybe she can help us."

"How?" Jagger asked.

The captain shrugged. "No idea. Gods aren't really my area of expertise."

The snake paused, looking through the bars at them. Her eyes glittered like starlight.

"She can't be a fan of the Aten, right?" Jagger's head was churning. "She must want the Aten banished so the power of the old gods will return. So why would she help the family that's trying to replace her and the other old gods?" Jagger didn't know much about gods, or their creatures, or whatever this was, but he figured some b-level goddess who was losing followers because of the upstart Aten would be happy to see him, and the family that promoted him, disappear from the scene.

"I'm not a fan of the Aten either, and I want to help us,"

Babi pointed out. "Neither are the two of you. Or Meretaten. Or Mut. Rejecting their god doesn't mean you reject the family, and it certainly doesn't mean you want to see innocent people murdered. Meretseger is a minor goddess, but she guards the royal tombs. She protects the royal family. Maybe she's just doing her job."

The priest kept calling out names and titles. After Mek, Herihor named family members in order, oldest to youngest. Jagger swallowed hard when Tatia's name was called out, and the priest shoved a stone into her wax figure's belly. Tut and the smaller princesses were named last.

"We have to do something," Aria whispered. "He's gonna kill them!"

Jagger gulped stale air. His sister was right, but it was impossible to think with the priest's baritone voice building like a sinister symphony, competing with the rush of the wind and the trill of the snake.

SSSsssssss!

"Can you get us out?" Aria dropped to her knees and addressed the snake.

Meretseger whipped her tail back and forth, like an agitated dog. She kept her distance from the bars of sand and smoke, unwilling, perhaps unable, to enter the cell.

"I name you enemy of Aten," the priest's voice rang out. Jagger looked up in time to see Herihor spit on a small, wax figure. He wrapped the figure's head in a strip of linen as he chanted. Enclosing the entire thing in clay, he molded it into a ball and scrawled on the outside with his reed pen.

SSSSSS! SSSSSSSS!!!! Meretseger's agitation grew.

Herihor dropped the ball, and Jagger's heart plunged down with it.

The High Priest lifted his foot. The wind paused.

"No," Aria whimpered.

Herihor stomped down, crushing the ball beneath his sandal.

The wind blew harder, and the red lights went crazy, dancing faster and brighter and higher, bouncing off the star speckled ceiling like waves crashing against Lake Michigan's shore.

"What just happened?" Aria squeezed Jagger's arm.

"Something bad." He felt nauseous. He glanced at Babi, and his blood turned cold. "He's killing them, isn't he?"

The captain nodded. "That was the youngest princess." Babi clutched his stomach.

An image of the little princess Jagger had seen at the palace played before his eyes. He'd smiled at her, reminded of a younger Aria. The idea that she'd just dropped dead hundreds of miles away because this evil priest broke a clay ball was horrifying.

"ENOUGH!" Babi's scream filled the small room, drawing the attention of the three men.

"Ignore him," Herihor ordered as he picked up another

small, wax figure. "I name you enemy of Aten."

The snake slithered back and forth, hissing angrily.

"Help us," Aria begged, tears streaming down her cheeks.

Jagger felt like his skin was on fire. He had to do something. But what? He stared at the goddess. "Our stuff!" he yelled. He pointed at Aria's purse, his phone, and Babi's sword. He had no idea how their stuff would help, but it couldn't hurt, and it was the only idea he had.

The snake placed her large, sleek body behind the stack of goods and slithered until Aria could reach their things.

"Distract them. Do anything," Jagger yelled.

The High Priest wrapped the wax figure he held in linen. Jagger grabbed his phone and started clicking his camera like a madman, remembering how awed Herihor had been by the flash. Blinding, white light erupted in the dim tomb, much brighter than the red lights dancing to the spell.

Aria lobbed what looked like colorful Easter eggs at the priest. It was her treasured lip-gloss collection.

The snake slithered off and disappeared as Babi banged his sword against the stone, yelling Egyptian profanities. The noise gave Jagger an idea, and he clicked to his music, selecting the first song that popped up and blaring it on high volume before returning to the camera.

Jagger's favorite hip hop song exploded in the tomb, bouncing off the walls and burying the other sounds in its base.

"Stop them!" The General pointed one finger at them and another at Smenkare.

"No! Don't move," Herihor yelled in response. He dropped the second clay ball, and smashed it under his feet.

Another death, like a sword to the gut.

Jagger aimed his camera at Herihor and clicked again.

"Keep going!" The old man's lips curdled in anger as he shielded his eyes with one arm.

The prince hesitated for an instant, glance shifting between the General and the High Priest, then he rushed toward the kids, murder in his eyes.

The moment the prince left the triangle's boundary, the wind died, and the red lights twinkled out. Jagger was so surprised he stopped clicking the camera, leaving the tomb lit by ordinary torchlight. Babi stopped banging the walls, and Aria was all out of lip-gloss to hurl. She clutched a handful of coins, clearly intending to throw them next. Jagger knew they'd been mined from her emoji-drenched change purse, which was always loaded to bursting with coins from countries across the globe.

Herihor's face turned purple with rage. He looked like he was seconds away from turning Smenkare into a frog.

Yeah, c'mon. Express yourself ... The song's rhythm built, filling the tomb.

"You idiot!" Herihor's face contorted, turning the handsome, old man into a creature of spite and anger.

The prince looked smug, like he was secretly pleased with himself. Had he meant to stop the spell?

"Resume!" the General shouted.

"Resume?" the High Priest spat back at the General. "Do you think a spell of this complexity can simply be resumed?"

Stand up. Lift the beat. Don't bring me down. Jagger clicked the song off, just as the priest stormed their way. The mist bars disappeared with a zap, and Herihor stomped in.

Babi shoved the kids backward and attacked Herihor with his sword. A sudden blast of steam materialized in front of the priest. It shielded him like a wall of impenetrable steel.

"You can't hurt me, sailor boy!" Spittle flew from the priest's mouth as Babi backed up, guarding the kids with his body. The General and Smenkare entered the small chamber and stood behind the priest. The room barely accommodated all six of them. Jagger stepped in front of Aria, adding a second layer of protection, although he knew it wasn't worth much.

"We should have killed you first," the General muttered softly, his nose flaring like an angry bull. His voice deep, like an old jazz singer's.

"I'll kill them now." Smenkare took a step toward them, apparently dying to be useful.

"You idiot!" Herihor turned on Smenkare. "We need nine, an Ennead. Nine family members are required for the spell to work. But because you," he said, and poked the prince. "Are too stupid to just stand still and let me do the real work, two of the nine are now dead."

Jagger felt like someone had shoved a hand into his chest and was squeezing his heart. Aria moaned. The youngest princesses really were dead.

The General growled, deep in his throat. He seemed to grow larger as he processed what the priest was saying. "Are you telling me you cannot cast the spell? Did you fail me?" It was said as a whisper, strangled and dangerous. As tough and magical as the priest was, Jagger saw a flash of concern cross his face and wondered what power the General had over him.

The High Priest's glance danced over Jagger and Aria. "No. I did not fail you, my General. Your idiot prince did. Again. But as always, I will fix it. I will deliver the throne to you, as I've promised. But we need these two alive. They are distant relatives of the family. The *Heqa-oo Moot* will be harder to cast with these two, rather than the princesses, but they will do. Fortunate that you have such a powerful magician at your side." He tossed a condescending look at the prince as he said this. "We need to start the spell over."

Jagger twined his fingers behind his neck, struggling to process what he was hearing. He and Aria were now the eighth and ninth family members, but that only meant they'd die sooner—it didn't change anything. Why wasn't Smenkare one of the nine? And how could the General get the throne if Smenkare was still alive? Certainly the king's son was in line before his General.

Jagger glanced at the prince. Smenkare looked pale. Was he surprised by this plan? He'd acted like he didn't know Herihor was part of the plot. Maybe that's why he'd stolen their letter of introduction. Why would he have done that if he'd known Herihor was on his side? Pieces began falling into place in Jagger's head.

"You can kill him though." Herihor nodded at Babi. "And bind these two. I do not want any more interruptions."

"I've got this." Smenkare pulled out a short sword as the General and Herihor stormed back to the tomb chamber.

Babi faced the prince, shoulders drawn back. If it weren't for Smenkare's magic, Jagger would have put his money on Babi in hand-to-hand combat between the two. The captain's body was longer and he seemed a million times tougher than the prince.

Holding his sword in one hand, the prince lifted the other, eyes darting back and forth as he faced the captain. "Stop."

Babi froze.

"Drop," the prince commanded.

The captain sank to the floor, his sword clanging to the ground. Babi lay, sprawled awkwardly as if he had no control over his limbs. The prince positioned his sword above Babi's neck. "Not so tough now."

A BALL AND PAIN

"Don't do it," Jagger pleaded, his head humming with adrenaline. He felt alive with energy, like lava was flowing through his veins.

It was the kind of buzz that hit him sometimes when the answer to a calculus problem was just out of reach. Jagger had no magic, no real powers but those granted to him by a necklace. He didn't even have Aria's purse. The one thing Jagger had was a mind that processed information quickly and accurately.

"They're going to kill you too." He stared up at the prince, connecting dots in his mind. "The General will take the throne. You thought it was yours. You didn't know Herihor would be part of this, did you? You thought you were casting the Death Spell. Did you really believe the General would work for you, a skinny, teenage pharaoh?"

Smenkare paused, lips pursed.

"Every member of the family has to die. Tatia saw it when she cast the *Meseneh Rek* spell to bring us back in time."

Smenkare's stare bore into Jagger. He tilted his head to the side, listening.

"Dude, you and I are like super distant cousins. Your half-sister said we'd cease to exist if the *Heqa-oo Moot* was cast. No member of the family will be left alive. If *we* can't exist, *you* can't exist."

The prince chewed his cheek, then glanced over at the General.

Jagger's chest tightened as Smenkare shoved a hand into the bag slung over his shoulder.

"Don't ..."

The prince pulled out a vial and splattered something wet and red over the captain. The drops multiplied, leaving Babi drenched in a blood-like liquid.

Still alive! Jagger swallowed, eyes glued to the prince.

"Now, for you two—"

"Don't hurt her. Please," Jagger begged. The request was ridiculous, and he knew it—this kid just murdered his own sisters.

Smenkare considered Jagger through narrowed eyes, then shifted his gaze to Aria. Jagger shifted closer to her, which was absurd—the prince just defeated Babi with a word. There was nothing Jagger could do to protect his vulnerable, little sis.

Smenkare grunted, then pulled a black, linen ribbon from his bag. "Bind."

The linen shot at Jagger, winding around him in an instant. He tossed his body, and the bindings tightened. He fell to the floor. Aria toppled down next to him, wrapped tight like a mummy. How had that tiny bit of linen covered them both so fully and quickly?

"Stop squirming," Jagger advised. "It makes it worse."

Aria blew a curl out of her eyes, glaring at the prince. Her entire body was covered in black, linen strips. Only her head was left free, like Jagger's.

"They'll kill you the second they get the chance. Herihor thinks you're a punk—"

"Enough!" Smenkare crossed his arms, staring at them a moment longer before pivoting and returning to the burial chamber.

Jagger wiggled, gently, in his mummy wrappings, trying to see what the prince was up to.

The High Priest hadn't bothered to block the door again, but Jagger's view was sideways. Herihor fished the two *Ka* stones from the shattered, clay balls, then plucked the others from the seven remaining wax figurines.

"Clean that up," the priest ordered the prince.

Smenkare bent over to pick up the shards. He glanced back at Jagger, jaw tight.

"He let Babi live," Aria sighed. "That's something."

Jagger shook his head. It wasn't enough.

Babi's eyes, the only thing on his body he could move, shifted from Aria to Jagger.

Jagger sucked in a lung full of air, then released it. What was the prince up to? "I don't know if he believes me," he whispered. "But he *would* be in line before the General. For the General to become pharaoh, Smenkare has to die. And he ruled for a few years. I read about it." Jagger swallowed. "Maybe I'm overestimating him. I was hoping he wouldn't feel like murdering his entire family for some other guy to get the throne. But who knows? Maybe he just wanted to be the one who killed his family."

Babi's eyes bore into him.

"Blink once if you agree, twice if I'm nuts."

The captain closed his eyes. Once.

Aria let out a long, slow breath. "Is he going to help us?"

"I doubt it. He just wrapped us up like mummies. But at least Babi's still alive. *He* might even survive the next hour."

"And the princess?" Aria's sob caught in her throat. "Is she alive still? Did he kill her?"

Jagger looked at the captain. One blink.

"I think he killed the two little ones we saw outside the palace. Not Tatia. And Herihor didn't stomp the big, green malachite stone yet. That one is Mek's. But none of us will be alive for long if we don't do something—"

"Come, Aten. Come to me." Herihor's chanting began again. Wind whipped through the tomb.

This time, they were bound tight: no more flashing lights, or flying lip-gloss, or sick beats. They'd overcome magical crocodiles, a giant scorpion, and even temporarily stopped a nasty, old High Priest and an evil General from murdering a boatload of their family members. But they were out of tricks.

Aria eyed her purse, a few feet away. Coins were scattered next to it. Babi's sword lay serenely on the ground.

"Your phone?" she asked.

Jagger sucked in a breath. It was in his right hand, bound to his side. His left arm was stuck to his chest, unmovable. Could he use his phone? He struggled to free his thumb and twist it so he could reach the screen.

"I've got it, but what am I supposed to do with it?"

"Anything!" she whispered loudly.

Jagger tapped the screen, trying to get anything at all to happen. Nothing. *Stupid passcode!*

"You depict the enemies of Aten." The priest was turning wax into bodies, one of which was Jagger's. Worse, another was Aria's.

Jagger knew, deep in his bones, that she'd be the next to die. Herihor had been murdering the youngest princesses first, maybe to work his way up to the most powerful. Jagger's fingers tapped frantically at his screen as he choked back tears. He couldn't watch his sister die, not even knowing he was seconds behind her.

The wind picked up, and the red lights winked off and on, bathing the cell in unnatural light.

"I'm sorry!" Jagger moaned. "I don't … I can't …"

"Poor Mom." Tears streamed down Aria's cheeks. "She'll never know what happened to us."

The noise that came from deep within Jagger was something between a wail and a moan. He didn't know he could make such a mournful sound.

Maybe he should tell his little sis he loved her or something. This would be his last chance. Looking at Aria, Jagger's brain reached for words. He should say something big, something important, before they dropped dead. But what could he possibly say?

He'd die seconds after her. That made it better for him, but it wouldn't help Mom, or Grams and Gramps, or Dad, or Tatia, or Mek and her family.

"I love you, Brainy." Aria blew out a puff of air. "It's not your fault."

Jagger couldn't see his sister—his eyes were too full of tears.

"The nine are assembled, the Ennead is created," Herihor screeched.

Blood coursed through Jagger's veins like lighter fluid.

"I name you enemy of Aten," Herihor wailed from the next room.

Jagger struggled against his bindings, desperate to stop the priest before another clay ball was smashed and his sister dropped dead next to him. The linen grew tighter around him.

The priest dropped the ball.

Time sped up.

One second, Jagger was trying to think of something, anything, to stop the old priest from killing Aria. The next, it was too late.

Jagger heard the crunch of the mud ball shattering, and Aria sagged, lifeless.

"Nooooo," Jagger wailed.

He closed his eyes and squeezed them tight. "No, no, no," he mumbled.

He opened his eyes.

She was still there, lying next to him. She was staring right at him, but her hazel eyes were empty, devoid of all the life and energy that animated his little sister.

Aria was gone.

"I'm sorry," he moaned. "I'm sorry. I'm sorry."

He squirmed closer to her—close enough to lean the top of his head against her shoulder. He was moments away from death himself. He welcomed it. This piercing pain would end. He didn't want to live with this failure.

He'd failed himself.

He'd failed Mom.

Worst of all, he'd failed his baby sister.

He took a deep breath, waiting. At least his pain would end now. He couldn't think about Aria, or Mom, for another second. It was too painful.

The High Priest's voice came for him. "I name you enemy of—"

CRASH!

Small bits of something dry and hard struck him, and he opened his eyes.

18

DA FEET

Jagger's vision was blurry. He blinked tears away, and a clod of dirt hit his forehead.

A black, metallic foot pierced the outside tomb wall. Above it, a gold hand shot through, sending more dirt flying.

Babi groaned.

Jagger watched in confusion, heart thumping, as the hand was followed by an arm, a leg, a torso, and, finally, a familiar looking, golden dog head with pointy ears. It was one of the large statues that had guarded Mek's mummy back in the tomb—the statue that had given him the creeps. It looked like an Egyptian themed robot from some crazy sci-fi film.

The dog-headed guard shook dust from its gleaming limbs, swiveling its head back and forth. Mut, covered in dirt, stumbled in behind it, through the hole they'd tunneled. She wore leather leggings and a simple shift that had probably been white before she burrowed into the tomb. Short braids hugged the scalp of her wigless head. Her bag of magical items hung at her side.

She took in the scene and gasped. "No."

She dropped to Aria's side, running her hands over Aria's face and bound body. Mut flicked her fingers, and the mummy bindings fell off Aria and Jagger.

He rolled over, pulling his sister to him. Aria didn't move. He put his hand on her heart, hoping. But there was no life there.

"Why are you stopping?" The General's voice boomed from the next chamber.

Jagger couldn't make out Herihor's response. He watched, heart aching, as Mut wiggled her fingers over Babi.

"Ahhh!" The captain shot up and charged out of the small chamber, holding his sword high. The metallic dog was right behind him.

Mut gripped Jagger, squeezing his shoulders tight. "I'm so sorry, Jagger." Tears swam in her eyes. "If the *Heqa-oo Moot* killed Aria, that means at least one princess is dead too. More will die if we don't stop this now. You need to gather the gemstones."

"I can't … I can't …" Jagger sobbed. He couldn't string three words together. How could he help fight an evil General?

He'd already lost the one thing he needed to protect. He'd failed in his most sacred responsibility.

"You can." Mut stood and yanked Jagger up. "If they win here today, Aria's death is in vain. You owe it to her to stop them now. If we don't, more people will die. Other wonderful, beautiful, little girls like your sister will die—"

"Ahhh!" Babi screamed.

Mut glanced at the door, then turned back to Jagger. "You don't know all the others who'll die, but that doesn't make their lives less precious."

"No," Jagger sobbed. "I can't."

"You can. For her, you can. Get the gemstones." Mut pulled Jagger toward the main chamber. "Now." She rushed in, wiggling her fingers and chanting, but Jagger stopped at the door.

It was as if a massive, pyrotechnics display had erupted inside the tomb. Lights were flying. Red lights battled purple lights. Green lights glittered around them as the wind thrashed.

Babi faced the General, sword clanging against sword, as they moved away from the sarcophagus toward the main door to the chamber. The General stepped backward, out of the magically drawn triangle, and some red twinkling lights faded. The din of clashing steel sounded even louder as the wind dimmed.

Smenkare scowled at the golden guard that faced him. The prince uttered clipped words, and green lights bounced off the guard's metallic surface. Smenkare tossed something on the ground, and a dozen snakes materialized, winding themselves around the guard's legs, binding them together. For a moment, Jagger thought the crazy, dog creature would tumble and crash, but it brushed the snakes away like it was swatting flies. They rustled in anger. One of the snakes transformed into Meretseger. She hissed, her long, lithe body dwarfing the smaller snakes, which slithered away from her like scared children running from an angry mother.

Smenkare stared down at the snake, his mouth hanging open. Taking advantage of the moment, the guard closed his fingers around the prince's throat and pinned him to the far wall. Meretseger slithered back and forth as if she approved of the guard's triumph over the prince.

Herihor laughed, and Jagger's gaze shifted to Mut. She faced the High Priest. They glared at each other like angry school kids in a competitive staring contest. Steam rose from Herihor's feet. It swirled around him like a cloak. Mut's fingers danced over the wax she held. The sounds of her chanting echoed off the walls, jarring with the thuds of clashing swords. Purple lights twinkled, and the smell of lotus blossoms filled the air.

Jagger sucked in a deep breath as a scarab beetle bloomed at Herihor's back. It was green and gold, about five feet tall. It flapped its wings and clacked its pincers, reaching for the priest.

Herihor whispered under his breath, arms waving, and red lights flashed on and off. Smoke streamed around his feet, quickly transforming into a ball. It grew, enclosing the priest inside of a misty, protective sphere.

Jagger looked back at Aria, the bitter taste of sorrow on his tongue. His throat was tight.

"You're no match for me, girl," Herihor sneered at Mut.

The sphere of smoke that enclosed the High Priest pulsed, kicking a clay ball toward Jagger. The ball rolled to a stop a foot away from him. On it were symbols of a snake, bird, jar stand, and mouth. Jagger knew the phonetic value of those signs. It read, *Jagr*.

"My gemstone," he whispered, glancing down at the ball.

"Ahh!" Mut screamed and writhed like she was on fire. Steam rolled off her body, mingling with the ball of mist surrounding Herihor. The scarab beetle shoved on the misty ball, rolling the priest until he was upside down in the orb. Herihor chanted louder. His head hovered above the ground, held aloft in the floating ball of steam with his feet in the air. The beetle shoved the mist orb, but the sphere couldn't get traction, and it rose farther off the ground.

Jagger stared back down at the clay ball. A wax figure of him, a gemstone stuck in the wax Jagger-doll's belly, was inside it. Would he drop dead if he crushed the ball? His sandal shifted closer. Maybe he didn't have to go back to Chicago without his sister.

He glanced back at Aria, wiping away tears and snot. She was too still, too lifeless, too dead. He felt cold all over. The ball of clay rolled closer, tapping his sandal. Maybe it wanted him to crush it. Maybe it was tempting him. And he was tempted. If it weren't for …

He heard his sister in his head, taunting him. *Think of Mek, Brainy! No time for analysis paralysis. Stop the evil slime ball!*

Jagger glowered at the High Priest, chanting away, upside down in his magical sphere.

"Okay, lil' sis," Jagger mumbled. He couldn't save Aria. And maybe he couldn't live with that. But before he figured that out, he might be able to hurt the man who'd hurt her.

Jagger scooped the clay ball up as Mut fell to her knees, moaning.

Go!

The gemstones were on the sarcophagus. He limped over, glancing at the others. Mut looked up at Herihor, floating above her in his sphere of smoke. She was chanting and crafting something from wax. Smenkare struggled against his captor but the guard had him easily in hand. The captain and General continued their sword battle, equally matched.

Jagger leaned on the sarcophagus. Seven wax dolls were lined up on top of it, tummies dotted with the gemstones that held Mek's *Ka*. He looked down. A large chunk of lapis lazuli sat on the ground, surrounded by a shattered, clay ball. *Aria!*

The world spun as he reached over to pick up the gemstone that represented his sister. He cradled it in his hand, feeling hollow.

Blinking away tears, Jagger set Aria's gemstone on the sarcophagus next to the wax figures. He put his clay ball next to it. He needed to gather the nine gemstones, but what if he hurt the family by plucking them out of the wax figures? His mind whirled. No, that didn't fit the evidence. The seven figures hadn't been spit on and wrapped in linen and rolled into a ball with their names scrawled on it. Only his had. And Aria's. That meant …

If Jagger could get his stone out without dropping dead, he could definitely get the others out.

"Screw it," he grumbled as he picked up his clay ball, took a deep breath, and smashed it against the sarcophagus.

He held his breath, waiting to drop dead.

No luck. He sighed, unwinding the little, wax Jagger and pulling a chunk of jasper from its belly. He set the jasper next to the lapis lazuli, then looked around for something to put them in. Where was the sack Smenkare had earlier? It was hard to see with the chaos of clanging swords and swirling smoke and the flashing lights from the magician's battle.

Jagger twirled in place. He spotted four large, limestone jars grouped together in a golden chest. The jar lids varied: one was in the shape of a baboon, another was a falcon, one was a woman, and the fourth, a jackal. Canopic jars, meant to store the organs of the deceased for the afterlife. Jagger grabbed the jackal headed jar and dumped out the contents. He didn't give a second thought to the remains of the old king's stomach, now cast carelessly on the ground.

"No analysis paralysis," he mumbled, grabbing gemstones from the wax dolls and shoving them into the canopic jar. When he got to the large chunk of malachite shoved into the biggest wax doll, he paused. "Sorry, Mek," he breathed as he pried it loose.

"AHHHH!!!" Mut screamed and doubled over in pain.

Jagger looked up, watching in horror as Babi, distracted by Mut's scream, turned toward her, giving the General the opening he needed. The General's sword pierced the captain's side. Babi fell just as Mut's body hit the ground, as if they'd synchronized their failure. Jagger had no idea how much of the blood covering the captain was from Smenkare's vial and how much was from the wound. But the captain was motionless. Dead?

Mut wailed louder. Whether it was because of the pain or because of Babi, Jagger couldn't tell. But she must have lost control: the beetle melted into the ground. The mist ball that held the priest vanished with a pop, and Herihor hit the floor, an evil smile blooming across his face as he righted himself and stood. The guard turned his dog head. He and Smenkare watched like spectators as the General and Herihor welcomed victory over Babi and Mut. The wind and lights vanished.

Jagger shoved Mek's gemstone into the jar with the others and clutched it to his chest like a football player cradling a ball near the end zone.

"You." Herihor turned his attention to Jagger. "Give me those gemstones."

The General stomped toward him. Babi's blood dripped from the General's sword, glittering in the torchlight.

Jagger's gut clenched. He eyeballed the door to the small cell where his sister lay. Could he make it to Aria? Maybe escape through the tunnel Mut and the guard had created?

"Now!" Herihor's voice was like a whip.

"Never," Jagger hissed. "You can't have my sister's gemstone!"

The General reached Jagger. He lifted his sword to Jagger's throat, a smile spreading slowly across his face. "Who's going to stop us?" His voice was cool.

Jagger squeezed the canopic jar. His hand grazed the Isis Knot amulet.

What?

His heart throbbed, and his eyes flew to the chamber door just as she walked in.

"Jagger Jones is going to stop you, General."

NOT TOO SHABTI

Tatia stood at the chamber's main door, behind Babi's body, with the second dog-headed guard from Mek's tomb at her side. The princess was dressed like a servant girl. Even in rags, power emanated from her like heat from a fire.

How did she get here? Jagger clutched the canopic jar tighter as the General's sword tip pressed against his throat.

"My children," the General hissed.

The dog-guard held a kid in each hand: a girl and a boy, wound in mummy wrappings and held by the guard like balloons on a string.

"Your children would like you to drop the sword." Tatia's calm demeanor was marred only by the worried glance she tossed at Mut, who moaned softly.

"Children," Jagger mumbled. That solved another small mystery. These must be the kids that had entered the temple complex earlier, delivering Tatia's letter of introduction to Herihor. Smenkare must have given the General the letter because he didn't know Herihor was on evil's side, and the General sent his own kids to warn Herihor. These must be the same kids Babi's sailors had followed to Amenhotep's tomb, presumably when they returned to report back to their father.

Jagger swallowed hard. This creep was a dad. And still he'd murdered Aria without a thought. He leaned into the General. The sword point dug deeper into his neck, stinging him. Hot, wet blood dripped down his throat and chest.

The General didn't notice. He glared at the princess, nose flaring.

Tatia smirked. "The difference is, General, he is not my child. If either of them dies, your only two children die also."

Jagger moaned. She didn't know Aria was dead. As if she'd just realized his sister wasn't here, Tatia's eyes roamed over the chamber, landing on Jagger. Tears stung his eyes, flowing down his face to mix with the blood. He pushed against the sword, letting it dig deeper, bite into his skin harder, and Tatia blanched.

She yanked the General's daughter closer. Would Tatia really kill the girl in retaliation? Or was it a bluff? She glared at Herihor, and Jagger believed she'd do it, especially if she'd just figured out her two youngest sisters had been murdered.

The General must have come to the same conclusion: the sword shifted away from Jagger's throat.

Herihor's hands whipped up, and steam billowed toward the princess.

Quicker than anyone had a right to be, Tatia countered. She flicked a finger, and the High Priest's wall of magical steam simply evaporated, vanishing with a weak zap.

Tatia had barely moved. Jagger recalled her bragging that she was the most powerful magician in generations. Herihor was no match for the princess, even if she was only a year older than Jagger.

The General dropped the sword and grimaced.

"You'll have other children, General," Herihor pleaded. "If you want the throne, you must make this sacrifice. If we lose here today, we will not get another chance."

The General gazed at his children, glancing from boy to girl. The boy looked scared, but the girl wore defiance like a shield. She stared at her dad with a curled lip.

"It is for them that I do this," the General responded. "It is for them that I want to return our country to the glory we once knew. It is for them that I want our family to rule the Red and Black Land, so we will be released from the power of the lunatic we call Pharaoh, to rule again as Egyptians should." He looked calm as his eye searched Tatia's. "You win today, little girl."

The princess smirked at the intended insult, but her eyes were angry. "My sisters?" Her voice cracked, and she lifted her head higher.

The General looked away. "It was the only way."

Tatia's hand flew to her chest as if she'd been punched. She hadn't known. Or perhaps she had, but the confirmation still hurt. She paused, then threw her shoulders back. Stepping into the chamber, she leaned down to check Babi's pulse before making her way to Mut. "Babi lives," Tatia whispered as she helped Mut stand.

Mut glanced back at Babi as Tatia reached into her dress and pulled out a small amulet. She cast it on the ground, lips hard.

The tomb was eerily quiet. The sound of Jagger's sniffles and the tinkling of the amulet hitting the ground were the only sounds as everyone watched the princess. First, she showed up out of nowhere. Now, she held attention as easily as a Chicago skyscraper held people.

Jagger eyed the chamber where Aria's body lay. *Aria!* His heart throbbed. His blood roared in his ears, loud against the silence of the tomb, now lit only by torchlight.

He squeezed the canopic jar tighter, aching to go to his sister. Herihor studied Tatia like a scholar, just a fellow magician anxious to learn a new trick.

Tatia closed her eyes and called to Osiris and Isis. A rainbow of lights exploded above the amulet. It was so small

Jagger couldn't make out the shape. The smell of eucalyptus and mint bloomed, and Jagger was reminded of watching the princess and the blinking Horus eye amulet. It seemed like years ago, yet it had only been a few days. He moaned, wishing none of this had ever happened. He should have stayed in that bed in Amarna. He should have ignored the voice calling out to him. He should never have put Aria in danger. She may have died anyway, but at least they'd have gone together, and he wouldn't be left with this crippling guilt.

He flinched when the amulet jumped with a *clink*. When it landed, three larger amulets lay on the ground. They jumped again, growing larger still. A few hops later and Jagger realized they were shaped like coffins.

"No." Whatever Tatia was up to, Herihor must have figured it out. He no longer looked interested. He looked terrified.

A few more hops, and three full-sized coffins sat before them.

"Father." The young boy struggled against the golden guard's steely grip, to no avail.

"He'll live," Tatia assured the boy. "For now. Which is more than I can say for my baby sisters. And his." She looked at Jagger and swallowed.

Dropping her eyes to the floor, she walked over to Jagger and bent down behind the large, red sarcophagus. When she stood, she held something in her hands. *Shabti.* Small, blue figurines of workers that were traditionally buried with ancient Egyptians so that they had someone to do things like gather food and pour drink for them in the afterlife. The six *shabti* were carved of faience, arms crossed over their small chests like mummies. There were three women and three men, each dressed to represent a different activity. One woman carried a basket of bread loaves on her tiny head, a man held a funerary symbol, and another had a sack filled with goods tossed over his little back.

"I can help." Mut limped over and took the *shabti* from Tatia's hands. Mut chanted, her fingers moving as purple lights danced around them.

Tatia pointed at the coffins, looking from Herihor to the General to her half-brother, still pinned to the wall by the dog-headed guard.

The General grunted. There was a hint of dignity in the way he held himself, walking to the coffin and climbing into it. He crossed his arms over his chest, mimicking the *shabti's* pose.

Herihor was a different story. He looked mad with fear. He mumbled under his breath and backed up against the far wall of the tomb chamber. At a nod from Tatia, the guard who held Smenkare dropped the prince in a heap, crossed the chamber to grab the old priest, and dumped Herihor unceremoniously into the coffin.

"Now you, brother," Tatia spat, pointing at Smenkare. "I'll let Father decide what to do with you, but until then you'll stay here under the care of the *shabti*."

"But I saved him," Smenkare whined. "I saved the captain. Ask him." The prince nodded at Jagger.

Jagger saw the General look up from the coffin, his serene acceptance of defeat marred by surprise. If he hadn't planned to kill the prince before, he did now. Tatia glanced at Jagger, and he bowed his head. It didn't matter anyway. None of this mattered now.

Tatia tapped a finger against her cheek, thinking.

Mut finished her spell, and the *shabti* sprang to life. Six small, blue figures clambered nimbly up the sides of the coffins, three to each, checking on the General and High Priest. Only a few inches tall, each scurried back and forth over the men. One of the girls appeared to be handing Herihor a miniature, blue fish as a snack.

A sob escaped Jagger's lips: Aria would have loved this. She should be the one here, watching magic, not him.

"Let me come with you," Smenkare begged. "Don't leave me with them."

"They'll kill him if they can." Jagger's voice was flat. The prince's life would be in danger if he were to be left. And in the timeline Jagger had learned from books, the prince ruled for a short period. It seemed like history should be kept intact. Why had his sister died, if not to keep history whole?

Tatia folded her arms, glaring at her half-brother before shrugging and bidding Mut to bind the prince along with the General's two children.

"My children?" the General asked. "What will happen to them and their mother?"

"I'm guessing they'll suffer the consequences of your traitorous deeds," Tatia said. "Pharaoh will decide. With my sisters dead, he will hear the truth. Finally. But for all your criticism of my father, he is fair and reasonable. He'll decide their fate, as he'll decide yours. Someone will return. Eventually. The *shabti* will keep you alive until then."

Three of the *shabti* worked together to close the lid over Herihor, whose scream reverberated through the tomb. The *shabti* swarmed the top of the coffin, busy doing whatever magical deeds they were charged with to keep the two men alive and bound in the coffins until the king's justice was decided.

Tatia's eyes met his. Jagger's gaze shifted to the small chamber where Aria lay. Dead.

The princess's chin quivered. "I'm sorry, Jagger Jones."

Bile crawled up his throat, choking him. Aria was gone. And he was still here.

"Our sisters deserved better." Tatia stared over at the small chamber.

Mut leaned over Babi, feeling for a pulse. "He'll live," she said.

SSSSSSSsss.

The Meretseger snake squirmed out of Aria's chamber, hissing.

Tatia's eyebrows shot up in surprise, then she bowed

reverently. Mut followed, bowing low as she clutched her side.

"Thank you, Silent One," Tatia said as the snake slithered around the coffins like a dog marking its territory. After a turn through the room, the snake stared at the princess, then Jagger, then slithered away.

"Meretseger," Mut breathed.

Tatia stared after her. "I've never … That's … Why?"

"She was here before." Jagger sighed. "She helped us earlier, and she was in the battle. She helped defeat Smenkare. Didn't you see her?"

Tatia and Mut shook their heads in tandem.

"That may be the most puzzling puzzle of all." Mut stared at the spot where Meretseger had been with her eyebrows knit together.

"Yes." Tatia sagged. "But that puzzle must wait." She glanced back at the chamber where Aria lay and hung her head. "Carry Aria Jones gently," she told the guard, who held the ends of the linen bandages that were wrapped around Smenkare and the General's two kids. He handed the ends to the other guard, who'd scooped Babi up in one muscular gold arm, and ducked into the room to get Aria.

Aria's body looked tiny in the guard's big arms, her legs and arms dangling down. Jagger limped after him. He could only see her feet; they jiggled with the big creature's gait.

He felt empty, like his insides had melted, as they filed through the tomb. Just after they passed the chamber with the well, Smenkare stumbled into him.

"Hey!" Jagger turned and shoved him. His blood was loud in his ears, and his skin felt hot. He glared at the prince, thinking of Aria, and of the two small princesses— Smenkare's own half-sisters—who'd lost their lives to this greedy madness. So much life snuffed out so suddenly, so senselessly. The anger that had erupted when they faced the giant scorpion flared. And now the anger had a target.

The prince righted himself and stabbed a finger in Jagger's chest. The vein in his neck pulsed. "I saved your captain. I helped you—"

"You murdered them!" Jagger roared. "You murdered my sister. You murdered your own sisters." Jagger dropped his voice. "I know what history has written for you, you lowlife scumbag. I'm from the future, remember? The fate coming at you might not be as gruesome as you deserve, but trust me, it's bad enough."

The prince stepped back. His eyes pulsed.

Jagger was lying. He knew the prince had died young but had no idea how—but the prince didn't know that.

Tatia pulled Jagger's arm, gently. "We need to go." She sniffled and turned to move forward.

Mut nodded for Jagger to follow as she shifted to stand between him and the prince. "We should have locked him in the coffin," she sneered as she pushed Jagger forward, out of the tomb.

STAY WOKE

Jagger was startled by the bright stars of deep night as the fresh air hit him—the stars put Amenhotep's painted tomb ceiling to shame. Aria would love it. That thought was like a punch in the gut.

"Stop," he mumbled. "I want to see her."

Tatia put her hand on the dog-headed guard. He was surprisingly gentle for an oversized, metallic creature as he set Aria carefully on the red, desert dirt in front of the tomb.

Jagger dropped to his knees next to his sister's body.

He draped himself over her. Sobs wracked him—he couldn't breathe. It didn't matter. Nothing mattered. He'd done his part. He'd helped lock the General and that vile traitor, Herihor, in coffins, alive. It didn't help his sister. He didn't feel one bit better.

"I'm sorry, Jagger Jones." Tatia's hand pressed against his shoulder.

He shook his head and hiccupped. She'd lost sisters too. He should give her back her amulet. He didn't need it. He didn't need anything anymore. He'd go home, tell Mom, then … what? He hiccupped again, pulling the amulet off. He clutched it to his chest, praying for his sister to come back. He'd be a better brother if only Aria didn't have to die. He'd never complain about her again. If only.

Jagger didn't believe in prayers. He'd always put his faith in science. But science didn't explain the powers of the necklace wound around his fingers. He'd learned that gods existed. Even a scientist had to acknowledge the divine when it slithered in front of him. "If you really existed, you could bring her back," he babbled. "You could prove you're real. You could give me another chance. Please."

The amulet seared his palm.

"Ah!" He shook his hand.

"Jagger Jones." Tatia's voice quivered. "Look up."

A light hovered above him. "What?" He flinched. Something was … Jagger looked down at his chest, and watched in shock as another light drifted out of his body and climbed up to jangle next to the first.

The *Seshep ny Netjer.*

"Two Gods' Lights." Mut stared up, fingers twined

behind her head. "Why? And what are they doing?"

Tatia shook her head.

Jagger kept his eyes on the lights. He leaned farther over his sister, but what was the point in protecting her now? He blinked away tears, struggling to see. Why had they …? He'd been … What if?

If ancient Egyptian gods were real, maybe Isis really had brought Osiris back to life. Wouldn't that mean she could do the same for Aria? He'd been praying when the lights … Maybe …

For the first time in his life, Jagger wanted to believe in miracles. An image of Grams nagging Gramps popped into his mind. *Faith is like happiness,* she'd said one Sunday when Gramps had refused to go to church, *you have to choose it!* She'd slapped the counter on the word "choose."

Jagger had never chosen faith. He'd never believed in anything not proven by science. But back in Chicago, everything was about science: soaring buildings, fast cars, computers and smartphones, a river that had been forced to reverse course, even the food was famous for its molecular gastronomy. But ancient Egypt was different. Not different like other modern cities—they had cars and architecture too, even the small and poor ones—but different in its bones, like it was made up of unknown gene strands.

With all the magic he'd witnessed over the past few days, anything was possible. In this moment, he believed that the same way he believed his heart was pumping blood through his tricuspid valve, or that J was the only letter not found in the periodic table.

"Please, Isis. Please bring my sister back." Tears streamed down his face. Mut and Tatia were crying too. The dog guards and their captives stood back, away from Jagger and the girls. Smenkare's mouth hung open as he stared up at the *Seshep ny Netjer*. Jagger closed his eyes, thinking back to how Tatia had addressed the gods. He cleared his throat, squeezing the amulet tight. "Come to me, Isis. Help me. Help my sister. Please."

A tug.

Jagger's faith bloomed brighter.

"Bring Aria back, Isis. Give her the gift you gave your husband, Osiris. Take my life if you need to, but bring Aria back. Please. I know you can."

Something was happening.

A sensation …

Jagger opened his eyes. He watched the lights. They seemed to be watching him back. One light shifted toward him. It paused, then flew into his chest. He gasped. What if the other …

The other light pulsed bright. Jagger held his breath. "Please, Isis. You have a sister too. I know you can—"

The light shot into Aria.

Aria!

He could feel her!

She gasped and opened her eyes.

"Aria!" Jagger fell onto his sister. Then realized he might be hurting her and sat up, letting his hands rest on her shoulders. His pulse was racing with joy.

She stared at him. Her eyes were blank—dark and dead and empty, like Lake Michigan on a cold, winter's night.

"Do you know who I am?"

She gaped.

"Do you remember your name? Do you know what year it is?"

She shook herself. "You didn't tell me the year, Brainy." Her voice was scratchy.

"You're you! How are you—?"

Aria covered her face with her hands and moaned. "Can we just *not* with the ten million questions right now?" She rolled onto her side.

"Yeah. Yeah, okay. Anything." Elation rushed through him. "I mean, you're alive!"

"And I'm ..." She pushed herself up onto her elbow, glancing around at the strange gathering. "I missed it." She shook her head at Mut and Tatia. "You guys are here." Her eyes drifted to Mut. "Guess you're not such a crappy Protector after all."

Mut's smile outshone the stars above.

Aria glanced back toward the tomb. "We won!"

Jagger wiped his nose. Everything was wet and gooey. "Yeah, lil' sis."

She pointed a shaky finger at the tomb door. "Why are those two sleazy, rat-poop balls still in there?"

Tatia knelt next to Aria. "How did you know—"

"Tatia locked them in coffins. Alliiiivvvve." Jagger wiggled his fingers, laughing.

"Safe keeping until we can deal with them," Mut added.

Jagger glanced at Tatia, saw her trembling chin, and paused. "Wait." He turned to her. "Your sisters too?"

The princess shook her head. "No. This gift is from the gods to you. Nothing like this has ever happened in our history—"

"Why now?" Mut tapped her cheek with her finger. "Why Aria? Why would the gods …"

The princess shrugged. "The gods are a mystery." She wrapped her arms around Aria.

Aria's eyes were wide. She stared, mouth open, over the princess's shoulder, patting her back, then shoved a braid away from her nose.

Jagger exhaled. He was trembling. "You okay?" What if this wasn't real? What if it didn't last? He reached out and put his hand on her head—it was warm with life.

"I'm …" She paused. "Different. But okay, yeah. I … hey!" Her eyes darted to Smenkare. "Why isn't Smell-kare locked in a coffin alive with those other snot-covered, dung pellets?"

Jagger laughed, then felt guilty. His sister had sprung from the dead, miraculously. But Tatia's little sisters were still back in Amarna, drained of all that life that filled them when he'd seen them, only a few days ago. And Mek's life was fading.

"Funny you ask about him." Mut glared back at the prince. "I was just thinking we might need a do-over."

"We *need* to get to Mek." Aria struggled to stand.

Tatia sagged. She reached her hands down to pull Aria up.

Jagger put his hand out. "She needs rest—"

"No." Aria jumped up and brushed the dust off her butt. "That last thing I need is rest. Mek needs us. Now, before it's too late."

Tatia sniffled, staring at her toes.

Jagger helped Aria balance, thrilled with the feel of her warm hand in his. She turned to him and sighed. Jagger took a deep breath, closing his eyes. His sister was safe. They had, in spite of the crazy odds, managed to stop the spell and save their own lives along with who knew how many ancestors. He pulled her in tight for a hug. They weren't done yet, but their lives were no longer dangling by a thin thread.

"When did Tatia show up?" she whispered. "And Mut looks like crap. I didn't know that was a thing. Where'd she come from? What happened to Babi? Why is Smell-kare—?"

"I thought you said no questions." Jagger released her, smiling down at her.

"No. I said *you* couldn't ask questions." She limped forward. "I died and came back to life. I get to do whatever I want."

"Uh, okay. How long is this royal princess routine going to last?"

"Well, since we now know I really *am* a princess, it might last a while. You should probably get used to it."

Jagger chuckled. He felt guilty for the happiness that flowed through him. Tatia's sisters were dead. And Mek was going to die soon, hopefully not before they got to her.

Aria must have read his mind. "Now," she said, leaning into him, her voice tired and tense. "Let's get these soul stones things to Mek so she can have her happy Death Life. Even I'm ready for chocolate chip cookies and TV!"

Tatia turned away, hands in tight fists at her side. Mut bit her lip, eyes scrunched in concern, as she watched the princess motion at the guards and walk into the night.

FUR-EVER AND EVER?

Jagger lay still, eyes closed, listening to the sounds of a sandstorm banging against the palace walls. The events of the previous day rumbled through his head, and he reveled in the fact that Aria was alive.

No one back home would ever know what they'd done— no one would believe their crazy tale. But he and Aria would know. They'd know what she'd been through and that they'd helped save one side of their family and a few thousand ancestors they knew nothing about, not to mention their long-lost relatives, the royal family of Amarna.

He shifted to his back, and his butt and thighs screamed in agony. Tatia had put them back on donkeys when they left the tomb, leading them past the temples and tombs of the West Bank to Malkata palace, four painful miles away. Aria had peppered him with questions until the moment they saw the massive, mud brick structure that had been the personal palace of Tatia's grandparents, Amenhotep III and Queen Tiye. It greeted them as dawn broke, and his sister fell silent.

They were welcomed by servants who seemed genuinely happy to see Tatia and Mut. They led them to Tiye's old quarters, a smaller palace within the massive walls that enclosed the entire complex. Some local bigwig put Smenkare and the General's two kids in custody, while a doctor attended Babi.

"Get up." Aria jumped onto his bed and smacked him with a … what was that thing?

He grabbed the roll of cloth away from her.

"We need to go. What if Mek dies before we get back?"

Jagger's eyes flew open. "What time is it?"

"Go time," she huffed.

"It's still dark." He groaned and rolled to the other side, away from his sister.

"That's just the stupid storm," she whined. "It goes on and on. We've been here almost a day. Tatia says we're stuck here until it passes. But what if it passes too late?"

"A day?" Jagger shoved himself up, glancing around at the palace walls, painted in wildlife: flowers and reeds and animals and marshes were everywhere. The décor extended to the floor, which had a river painted on it—it reminded Jagger of the fish that swam across Tatia's bedroom floor. The ceiling and windowsills were covered in vines, and flying birds adorned the upper walls. "Where are they?" He pulled a linen blanket around his shoulders.

"Tatia checked in earlier. I can hear Mut next door, talking to Babi."

"How is he?" Jagger's donkey was behind Babi's last night, and he was sure the captain—bound to the donkey by one of Mut's magic spells—would drop dead on the ride.

"He's talking back. So that's good, right?"

Jagger rubbed his sore thighs as he stood, and stumbled toward the bedroom door.

Aria handed him some kind of cone-shaped bread slathered in honey. "It's amazing. Tatia left it." She flashed a quick grin.

He gobbled it up and grabbed another from a platter on a small gold table. He limped barefoot down the hall, Aria at his side, following the mumble of voices. Wood beams, painted green, held the ceiling aloft. Colorful, geometric patterns covered the ceiling, and the smell of cedar filled the air.

He paused at the first door. Three voices. He knocked, and Mut opened, waving them in with a tight grin.

The bedroom was decorated like the other one, but it was larger and richer. Babi sat up in bed, bound with mummy wrappings like the ones that had trapped Smenkare and the General's two kids last night, but whiter and cleaner looking.

He must have been okay, because he smiled at Jagger and Aria.

Tatia sat at the end of the bed, and Mut stood near the captain's head. The two dog-headed guards stood on the other side of the bed. They looked even bigger here than they had in the tomb.

"Congratulations are in order," Babi drawled. "You saved the gemstones." He nodded at the gold and alabaster table next to his bed where the canopic jar sat. Babi's smile faltered—Jagger guessed he was thinking of the moment Herihor dropped those balls and they knew they'd failed the two youngest princesses.

And then, later, Aria.

At least that part had a happy ending.

"Yay, good guys." Aria clapped facetiously, then stopped, twining her fingers together. "But that party's over. The gemstones won't help Mek unless we get back quickly."

"That's truer than you know, Aria Jones." Tatia pursed her lips. Dark circles rimmed her eyes, and she looked angry. "I'm afraid …" She dropped her head in her hands, sagging.

"We were just talking about Mek." Mut slipped down onto the bed, tossing a worried look at Tatia. Mut had obviously found time to bathe. She was stunning again, with a black wig studded with beads and amulets on her head and a transparent, gem-studded shift hanging to her knees. Sandal straps wound up her calves, and thick, golden bracelets circled her upper arms.

"I need a bath," Aria mumbled.

Looking at her scraggly clothes and hair, Jagger smiled. There were more challenges in front of them, but his little sis was safe by his side, worrying over her personal fashion, dirty and messy, like a normal, eleven-year-old girl. "You really do. You stink."

Aria socked him playfully in the arm then flashed him a dimpled smile. It felt good. "Focus!"

Tatia stood and began pacing. She was still dressed like a servant girl—a servant girl with perfect posture. Even in rags, she had the grace of a ballerina and the strength of a ninja warrior. "Travel is impossible while this storm rages. We can't sail the Nile in this, not today and probably not tomorrow." She pivoted. "Who knows how long it will last? Even if we left right now, there's no way get to Amarna in time. Maybe I shouldn't have ..." She whirled again, her feet slapping angrily against the marble floor.

"How did you get here?" Jagger put voice to the question that had been in his head since Tatia's sudden appearance as his neck swiveled back and forth, tracking her.

She twirled, rubbing her arms like she was cold. "I learned my half-brother had nabbed you two from Wenher, and tossed you onto Babi's ship. I guessed Smenkare was working with the General. I didn't want to believe it." She paused and leaned against a brightly colored pillar. Her voice was low and sad. "His hatred for our father is so intense it blinds him.

213

It's like a plague he carries in his heart. Father pays so much attention to us girls and treats the boys like they don't matter. Of course, my sisters and I are the queen's children. Father's other wives are no match for Mother."

"Right," Jagger mumbled. She had a point. Even the modern world had numerous images of Tatia and Mek, and their younger sisters, in museums across the globe. But the two boys, Smenkare and Tutankhamun, seemed like an afterthought. Sure Tut was famous in the modern world, but that was only because of his tomb. As magnificent as it was, scholars believe it was poor by pharaonic standards. Jagger once read an article that claimed the shift to a single, male god left a void, because Egyptians had worshipped goddesses for thousands of years. So Akhenaten tried to replace the old goddesses with his daughters. The thought reminded him again that two princesses were dead, and the rock in his gut hardened.

"I didn't want to leave Mek." Tatia pushed herself away from the pillar, and paced again. "No one but me can mix the elixir, and the potion only lasts a few days. But I had to come. If I hadn't, more people would …" She rubbed her brow. "If we don't get home by morning, Mek will …" She looked down, blinking fast, then marched faster. "It's impossible. What have I done?" She moaned.

"One day?" A wave of nausea washed over him.

"Why are we sitting here? We've got to go." Aria stomped

a foot. "But if it took three days to sail here ..." She glanced at Jagger, biting her lip.

Tatia wiped away a tear. "I made my choice. And my sister will pay for it."

"You did the right thing. If you'd have stayed, Mek would be dead already, along with the rest of your family." Mut reached out a hand and set her fingers on Babi's arm. "We can't give up now."

"I thought you couldn't leave the palace?" Jagger knew Mut was right—they couldn't give up. But he had too many questions swirling around in his head to concentrate on solutions.

"I cast the *Iroo Horou* and spelled my favorite handmaiden to look like me. I gave her instructions on how to give Mek the remaining elixir. Then, disguised as my own handmaiden, I walked out of the palace and jumped onto the fastest ship."

"You just ... like, swapped places?" Aria tilted her head to the side. "Because that's awesome. Can we do that—?"

"Aria," Jagger groaned. This wasn't the time.

Mut's eyebrow crawled up, and she drawled, "No one in Egypt can cast the *Iroo Horou* like Meretaten, but how would that help?"

"And we don't change places, Aria Jones." The princess paused and shook her head. "Just faces."

"Okay. But if you can do magic like that, why can't you just magic up something to stop this storm?" Aria crumpled her nose. "We have to get home. By tomorrow morning! Failure is not an option. You have to believe we can do this."

Tatia dropped her head in her hands. "I wish I could."

"Wind is my natural magic," Mut said, voice flat. "And even I can't do anything with a storm like this. Or drive a ship fast enough to get to Amarna in one day, even if it weren't for the storm."

"Did you know about Herihor when you entered the tomb?" Jagger needed to clear up some of the questions cluttering his mind so he could think straight.

Tatia looked up, eyes flaming like they might spit fire. "I did not, Jagger Jones. I had no idea until I saw him there with the General. I believed we could trust him. He and I have been allies my entire life. I can't understand why he did what he did. Sometimes power corrupts, and a man like him losing power he's held for so long …" Her voice trailed off, and she stared at a tree, painted on the far wall. "Father's efforts to rid our land of the old gods has had consequences he could never have foreseen. And now my baby sisters are gone. And Mek …"

The death of the two girls sat heavy on the room. The threat to Mek even heavier.

One day. Jagger felt sick. But Mut and his sister were right: they couldn't give up now.

"How long are Hemet and Mutef going to stay like that?" Aria interrupted the moment of silence.

Jagger turned his head to one side, then the other. Where were Mut's guards anyway?

Aria stared up at the guard dogs.

"Wait. You mean *they* are Hemet and Mutef?" Jagger asked. He looked at them, aghast. "But we saw them in the tomb in our own time. How could …"

Tatia narrowed her eyes, ignoring Jagger as she stared intently at Aria. "How do you know they are Hemet and Mutef?"

"I can feel them." Aria shrugged.

Tatia folded her arms. "The same way you felt Herihor and the General in the tomb," she mused. "Feel them how?"

"Not sure." Aria shook her head. "One second I was, well, dead, I think. Then I woke up, and I could sense you and Mut near me, and Hemet and Mutef, and Smell-kare. And Brainy, of course. I could feel those two pustules of vomit, the General and Herihor, back in the tomb. When I looked at Hemet and Mutef, they looked like that." Aria nodded at one of the statue dogs. "I assumed they'd be normal by now. How long will they stay that way?"

Tatia's eyebrows crawled up as Aria spoke.

Mut tilted her head to the side like a curious puppy. "Perhaps the *Seshep ny Netjer* gifted her some of the amulet's powers when it joined with her."

Tatia nodded, examining Aria. "Did you see the gemstones when you were in the tomb, Aria Jones?"

Aria nodded. "Yeah, I saw them."

The princess stared into space as if she was doing calculus in her head.

"You haven't answered my question," Aria added. "How long are Hemet and Mutef going to be robot dog things?"

Jagger touched the amulet. "I feel them too."

"Yeah." Aria scoffed. "Way to catch up."

Tatia turned back to Jagger and Aria, lips tight, but she didn't respond.

Mut grinned sadly at the two guards, large and silent next to Babi's bed. "They'll stay that way so they can guard Mek, if everything goes according to the plan."

"Uh," Jagger stammered. "You mean Mutef and Hemet were the guards from our time? They'd been that way for thousands of years?"

Tears glittered on Mut's eyelashes, but she blinked them away.

"You turned them into giant, robot dogs … forever?" Aria hunched up.

Mut nodded as the transformed men stood silent, watching them.

"Forever, forever?" Aria seemed as shocked as Jagger felt.

"For as long as they're useful in this form," Mut confirmed.

"Useful?" Aria glanced at Jagger. "Did she just say useful?" She turned back to Mut. "You don't *own* them. Their lives aren't yours to just throw away." She looked at Jagger again.

"Are they?"

He shook his head. For all he knew, these new friends of his were a bunch of slavers—he had no idea if the many people who worked to support the royal family were well-paid executives or lowly slaves.

"Stand down." Babi held up a hand, one side of his lips curved up good-naturedly. "Believe me, no one tells Hemet or Mutef what to do. They are their own men."

"I'd never have asked this of them." Mut reached out a hand and placed it on the black and gold guard nearest her. "I'd have stopped them if I could have. But as you say, they're not my personal property. They've been my guards, my companions, and my friends for my entire adult life and most of my childhood. It was Hemet who held my hand when my side lock of youth was shaved off. It was Mutef who rubbed my back as I cried myself to sleep when my first love left me for another. I'll miss them more than I can say. But they chose this fate. They offered themselves to Meretaten when she showed up, looking for a way to tunnel into the tomb. I honor their choice."

"How?" Jagger studied the guards, both repelled and fascinated. "How did you do it?"

Tatia squinted like she was surprised by the question. "I'm a magician, Jagger Jones. A very good one. I thought I'd explained that already."

"Can you make anything? I mean, can you create whatever

you want?" Jagger leaned forward. His brain was humming.

Tatia took a breath, then started explaining, like a teacher talking to a class. "Egyptian magic works in various ways, but it has limits. All magicians have a natural ability."

"Except for Meretaten," Mut interrupted. "She has several natural abilities."

"And some of us pick up new skills easily, while others can't learn anything they aren't naturally gifted with," the princess continued as if Mut hadn't spoken.

"Also, except for Meretaten. She can learn anything. Seriously, nothing stumps her!"

"But in general," Tatia said, crossing her arms. "We can't just create whatever we want from scratch. But we can *transform* things. We can increase the characteristics something already has, making something *more* of what it already is."

"Like I can transform a wax figure of a snake into a real snake," Mut explained.

"Magic of that type is short lived." Tatia began pacing again. "Wax is a blank slate. It has no magical properties, so we can create anything from it, but it's not strong enough to last long because it has no characteristics to enhance." Pivot. "It's a useful but fleeting magic, allowing us to create any reasonable form that exists in the world, but its power is limited and expires quickly." She paused, then resumed her march. "The magic I performed on Hemet and Mutef is bigger, stronger, and, well, in this case, exceptionally long-lasting. That's because they already *are* proud guardians. I simply enhanced their natural attributes. This kind of magic is much more complicated. I dare say, I'm the only magician in Egypt who could have done it."

"So why can't you just transform a boat so it's strong enough to sail through this storm?" Aria asked.

The princess looked confused by the questions, pausing for a moment before responding. "No magic can change the weather, and no ship, regardless of how strong, could sail the Nile in this. Storms like this are rare but unpredictable. There's no way around it." She leaned against the column again, closing her eyes in grief.

"No power in the world could speed this storm up, or enable us to sail through it." Babi sighed.

"Maybe we don't need to sail *through* it." Jagger lifted his chin high. "Maybe we can sail *over* it."

22

THAT'S CHARMING

"Over it? That's impossible." Babi sat up, then grabbed his head and lowered himself back down to the bed with a groan.

"Not really." Jagger's mind was purring, ticking through possibilities.

"Yeah," Aria exclaimed, jumping to his idea like only a girl who'd logged a million flight hours could. "If you wanted to create, say, a flying ship, could you do that with wax?"

"A flying ship?" Tatia shook her head. "I can't imagine such a thing, Aria Jones." She crumpled her eyes in concentration. "I could create a wax bird, but it would fall out of the air within a few miles."

"Okay." Jagger nodded. "What if you had something

stronger, like real birds? Could you transform them into something like Hemet and Mutef? Giant, robot birds that could fly farther?" Jagger knew that flying over the storm was the solution they needed—they could be back at Amarna tonight if only they could figure out how to merge his knowledge of flight with their magic.

"I could enhance birds, make them larger and faster and able to fly farther. But I couldn't control them. Birds are their own creatures. And why would I want to, Jagger Jones? To what end?"

"You want to fly to Amarna? Like in an air ship?" Babi twined his fingers above his head. "Even if that were possible, how would that be any safer than sailing by boat? You'd still need to sail against the storm, only you'd do it from the sky rather than on the river. Seems *more* dangerous."

"No." Jagger shook his head. "We just need to rise above the clouds. Thunderstorm clouds can get pretty high though—cumulonimbus cloud peaks can reach twenty thousand feet. So we have to get very high, very fast. Once we rise above the storm, we can fly over it."

"Over it?" Babi squinted.

"We do it all the time." Aria waved away his concern, nonchalant. "We've flown all over the world and through all sorts of storms. Why can't we just hop on a magical, flying boat and fly it to Amarna? Airplanes are way faster than ships. We ought to know, we've spent enough time in both."

Mut and Tatia exchanged a confused glance. Jagger was struck again by the power of modern science—these guys may have some cool gods and magic, but technology was pretty magical too.

Tatia played with a braid, eyes narrowed. "Even if we figured out how to control a bird, wouldn't it be too heavy? How would it stay in the air?"

"Well first, you need thrust." Jagger and Gramps loved to discuss the mechanics of flight. When Jagger was four, Gramps, who flew planes for the military in his younger years, taught him how to make paper airplanes. Surprised that Jagger's plane flew farther than his own, Gramps asked how he'd done it. When Jagger explained lift and thrust and drag, Gramps called him whiz kid—it was the first time anyone ever labeled Jagger that way—and talked Grams into making Jagger's favorite salted caramel, homemade ice cream. He'd been called a whiz kid a million times since, but most people used it like a slur, like it was a bad thing to be smart. Not Gramps though. Gramps thought it was the coolest! "To understand how thrust works, first you need to know—"

"ZZZZZZZ." Aria mimed falling asleep, then opened one eye, and aimed it at Tatia. "The same way birds stay in the air."

"Birds are birds, Aria Jones. Birds fly. I could transform a bird into something large enough to carry us easily enough— Mut and I both excel at altering sizes—but I can't force a bird to follow my commands."

"Okay." Jagger was shutting down options, looking for an idea that would work. "So wax isn't strong enough, and birds won't take orders. What other kinds of substances can you transform? There must be something with the right magical properties—"

"Perhaps …" Mut's smile was wicked. "Perhaps something stronger than wax but still biddable, something without its own will but with the form of a bird. Something made of a substance our princess masters exceptionally well?" She was playing with her hair. Pulling something from her braids, she opened her hand.

Aria gasped and clapped her hands together. She dropped her purse on the ground, and rummaged thought it until she plucked a charm from her charm bracelet stranded in the bottom of her bag. She added her piece of jewelry to Mut's palm.

Tatia bit her lip. "Yes. I could do that. But it won't help Mek if we fall from the sky to our deaths—"

"We won't," Jagger assured her.

"The storm—"

"Will be uncomfortable, but we'll get past it."

"But won't the sun scorch you?" Babi's eyes were wide with fascination.

Jagger chuckled. "No. In fact, the cold will be one of two problems we'll face once we climb past the storm—"

"What do you mean cold?" the princess asked. "That's

preposterous. We'll be closer to the sun."

"That's not how it works," Jagger assured her. "It's cold up there. But we have an even bigger problem. Depending on how high we have to fly to get above the clouds, we may get altitude sickness. There's less oxygen in the air as you get higher. If we go too high, we'll all be bumbling idiots. We could pass out if we get over eighteen thousand feet, and this storm may be that high. But maybe …" Jagger tapped his fingers against his arms, thinking about the time he and Andrew made homemade space helmets. "I needed a hose, water, some kind of big bubble, lots of extra clothes, and an airtight container."

Cold wind stung Jagger's face that evening as the sun fell in the sky. It had taken hours for him to figure out the science, and another for Tatia to cast her "truly brilliant, magic spell."

Tatia had created the giant falcon Jagger and Mut rode out of a golden Horus amulet Mut plucked from her wig. Their bird—Jagger had mentally named him Caesar—was gleaming gold, like the amulet had been. Jagger admired the beating, gold wings as he gripped the strap tighter. The leather strap was wrapped around the giant, metallic bird, holding him and Mut in their seats and allowing them to steer. Caesar's wings creaked as they moved up and down, then fell silent when he paused, gliding on the currents.

Aria and the princess flew next to them on a pink and purple owl with glittering, yellow eyes. Mom had bought Aria the charm near the Acropolis in Athens, one of many charms added to Aria's bracelet over the years from around the globe, this one to honor the goddess Athena's passion for wisdom, symbolized by the owl.

Jagger looked down, hoping to spot the Nile below them, but all he could see was storm clouds. Getting over the storm had been nerve wracking. And once they did, he'd wondered if his creative adaption of papyrus reeds, alabaster jugs, and an old tic-tac container from Aria's purse—used to create ad hoc oxygen tanks in case they got high enough to need them—would be enough. Fortunately, it was. Mut and Tatia both sucked oxygen every ten minutes or so as they cruised along at about fifteen thousand feet, if Jagger's estimate was right.

Tatia yanked her top layer of clothing tighter around her and leaned closer to the owl. She wore layers of white linen, her black, side ponytail peeking out from the cloth wrapped around her head. She looked nervous, glancing down and mumbling to herself. Maybe they'd found the one thing their tough princess was scared of: heights. It didn't help that she refused to believe Jagger's explanation of oxygen and weather patterns and the mechanics of air travel. Her disapproval of scientific facts reminded him of his own unwillingness to believe in anything magical—a belief that had collapsed in the face of spell after spell.

In the end, Tatia was so attracted to the idea of getting home in time to save Mek's *Ka*, her fear wasn't much of an obstacle.

Next to her, Aria's grin didn't stop. Jagger could hear her in his head: *this is better than the time we zip lined in Costa Rica, or went dog sledding in Scandinavia!* He smiled, watching his little sis enjoy the storm clouds twist and turn below them.

"I don't think you could have convinced Meretaten to ride that thing for anything, or anyone, other than Mek." The wind carried Mut's voice back to him. He dodged the loose end of the linen band wrapped around her head. "The sisters have always been close."

"We'll make it in time, right?" Jagger had done the math over and over again. They should be fine, now that they'd conquered the storm, but what if Mek was gone when they got back? What if the servant Tatia left in charge hadn't administered the elixir properly? Or the princess had been wrong about how long her sister could hold on?

"We'll make it." Mut sounded confident.

The clouds parted, and Jagger caught a glimpse of the green strip of fertile land that bordered the Nile. A surge of homesickness stabbed him. He closed his eyes, imaging the too-familiar view of Chicago from the sky, the vastness of Lake Michigan and the skyscrapers stretched out along it, and the grid of streets and neighborhoods fanning out from the city. *Home.* They'd be there soon.

He cleared his throat. "What about Babi? Will he be okay?"

"He's under Meri-Ptah's care. She's the best healer in the land. He was devastated he couldn't join us though. Sailing through the air is exactly the kind of adventure that appeals to our dear captain."

"And Hemet and Mutef? Won't you miss them?"

"Desperately." Jagger heard the wistfulness in her voice and understood that the sacrifice had been hers as well as theirs. "I always miss my companions when they're not with me. But they've made their choice. They can hardly drive me around on my chariot now. They'll make their way to Amarna as soon as Babi is ready to travel."

"What's going to happen to the General, and Herihor, and Smenkare?" Jagger had no idea what kind of punishment they'd face. Did ancient Egypt have cozy, white-collar prisons or would they be tortured and burned at the stake? If his knowledge of history panned out, Smenkare at least had more time, but what of the other two men?

Mut mumbled something about the king's dedication to peace and the warmth of love and honor, and the two of them fell silent.

"How long until we land?" she asked a while later as the moon climbed the sky. He'd tried to explain it, but neither Tatia nor Mut really understood the notion of sky travel. They didn't seem to believe they could get to Amarna so quickly.

"I think we passed Abydos about an hour ago, so, at this speed, probably two hours more." He'd calculated the speed of the birds and the distance of the flight, shorter now that they could chart a direct path.

"The palace will be sleeping, but the sentries will get a good shock." Her laugher was like bells, floating away on the wind.

They fell silent again, listening to the sounds of Caesar's flapping wings, buffeted by the wind, Aria and Tatia flying by their side, until Amarna appeared like a spot on a map, dark and silent. They'd left the storm behind and spent the last leg of the flight watching the meandering river sparkle far below as a bright moon filled the sky, surrounded by stars.

Jagger's stomach churned as he looked down on the peaceful city.

They were too late for two princesses. But another would be waiting.

He hoped.

PURR-TING COMPANY

The birds stretched their metal wings, gliding on the wind. The palace emerged from the dark. It was miniature at first, but the straight lines of roads and walls grew quickly, gleaming in the moonlight as they descended. It was an hour before dawn when Tatia ordered her pink and purple owl to land in the rectangular, open space next to the palace.

Rubbing his sore legs, Jagger followed Tatia through the maze of waist-high altars. Was that blood? He cringed, wondering how many cows had been slaughtered in this place. He was suddenly relieved he hadn't eaten hamburger recently.

They paused at a palace side door, looking back at the birds. The falcon flapped its wings and took off. Caesar didn't spare them a glance. The owl, however, watched them with yellow eyes before hooting and following Caesar into the starry sky.

"We should have taken them home." Aria grinned at him. "Can you imagine? Best pets ever."

He bumped her playfully, shaking his head. He and Aria had been begging Mom for a dog for years. She refused, blaming her job, which was one more reason to dislike Mom's travel schedule.

"Let's go." Tatia waved them forward. She led them through cold, stone, palace halls, dodging the few guards and servants that were up. Ten minutes later, the princess fell onto her bed next to Mek.

Still alive. Jagger unclenched.

By the looks of it, she was barely hanging on. Rather than the peaceful sleep of their previous visit, Mek struggled to breathe. Sweat dotted her brow, and her face looked sallow. Black moons curved under her eyes.

"It's time." Tatia ran her hand over her sister's bald head.

Aria sniffled as Mut pulled the canopic jar from her bag and spilled the nine gemstones onto the white bedcover. The stones sparkled in the dim light. The glow of magic animating them and illuminating the room cast an eerie light on Mek's face.

Tatia reached out and grabbed Jagger's hand. "Thank you, Jagger Jones. The gods were right. You saved my sister's *Ka*. You saved my family."

"*We* saved *our* family," Aria corrected her.

Jagger stroked his throat—he felt nauseous looking down at Mek, so much like Aria. But unlike his sister, Tatia's wouldn't survive the day. "I didn't ... I mean, I still don't understand ..."

"They chose you for a reason," Tatia replied, reading his thoughts.

He exhaled. "But you're the one who showed up in the nick of time and saved us—you and Mut. I would have failed if it weren't for—"

"We would still be in Thebes if it weren't for you, Jagger Jones." She released his hand.

"We'd be crocodile food by now if it weren't for you, Aria," Mut added.

"My sister would lose not only her life, but her afterlife. And your sister would be dead if you hadn't discovered the faith to revive her," Tatia said.

Would she?

Mut smiled. "You stood up to the General even when you believed your sister was gone. That took courage. And a kind of self-sacrifice that's not easily found."

Aria squeezed his arm. "Yeah, that was okay work, Brainy." Then she looked down at Mek, swallowing hard. "We've come this far. But we haven't helped Mek yet. We need to do this before ..." Her eyes darted to Tatia.

"Yes, Aria Jones. You're right. Again." Tatia sighed and

pulled the blankets down to reveal the *ankh* sitting on Mek's stomach.

Wordlessly, the two magicians shifted to stand across from each other, one on each side of Mek's head. They spread their arms, fingers nearly touching, over Mek's body.

Aria grabbed Jagger's elbow, tugging him out of the way. "She'll still be alive. Kind of." She sniffled.

Jagger put an arm around her, surprised to realize he agreed. He didn't even believe in an afterlife, but somehow, here and now, he knew this was not the end of Mek.

Mut and Tatia each selected two stones and held them in their outstretched palms. Mek's malachite sat on the bed next to her.

"I am Isis," Tatia chanted.

"I am Nepthys," Mut added.

"I am Selket," the princess continued.

"I am Neith," Mut finished.

"We call on the *Ba*," they chanted together. "We call on the *Ka*. We call on the *Ba* and *Ka* to unite, to join with the Heart, the Name, and the Shadow, to come home to the one to whom they belong."

Wind struck Jagger's skin as colorful lights erupted around the room. The birds painted on the walls looked like they were moving in the lights that sparkled and danced across the space.

"Mint *and* lotus," Aria whispered.

"We call you, Osiris. We call you, Anubis. We call on the Devourer to watch on, as the feather is weighed against Meketaten's heart and she is found pure. We call on the gods of old to take her to you, to welcome her home." The wind whipped harder as the lights spiraled up then down, like fireworks.

"Wisdom," Tatia chanted.

"Health," added Mut.

"Energy."

"Vitality," finished Mut.

They repeated the chant nine times. It became harder to hear as the noise of the wind rose higher and higher. When the mantra finally ended, the wind shot toward Mek, pulling the lights into her. Jagger pulled Aria close, covering his head with his other arm. They were pelted by hard air. It was like no storm he'd ever endured ... and that was saying something coming from a Chicago kid.

The wind died suddenly, leaving Jagger feeling bruised and battered. He dropped his arm to see the two magicians in the same place, arms out, hands empty. The gemstones had attached themselves to the *ankh*. The large, green malachite sat in the middle, the others scattered around it, looking just as it had when Aria reached out to touch it in the tomb. But this time the gemstones were truly there, no longer a mere vision.

Jagger gasped as a vivid, green light drifted up from Mek's body.

"Whoa." Aria's hand flew to her mouth, and she leaned into him.

The light pulsed with energy, hovering above Mek, vivid and intense. It was like the *Seshep ny Netjer*, but even brighter and green. Was it aware? Jagger had the sense that it was taking stock of the moment.

It shifted higher, and Tatia lifted a hand as if to greet it, or perhaps, wish it well on its journey. The light pulsed bright one time before drifting off, up and away through the blue ceiling peppered with gold stars.

"It's done." Tatia slid onto the bed. "Mek is with the little ones now."

Jagger felt weak. He watched Mut stroke Tatia's head with one hand and Mek's with the other, tears streaming down her face. "You have a sister still, and she'll need you more than ever. As Mek watches over the little ones, you must watch over Ankesenpaaten. And Tut."

Meow.

"Kitty!" Aria stepped instinctively toward the large, black cat standing at the open wall, front feet inside and back feet outside. It looked suspiciously like the cat he'd seen on the way to the airport in Chicago, and the cat Aria had befriended in Amarna.

Aria froze a few feet away from the cat.

"Uh." Jagger blinked, wondering if this was real.

"It grew." Aria stepped back toward him.

The cat was suddenly far larger than any cat had a right to be, sleek with fur that sparkled like the gemstones. It was magnificent, like nothing Jagger had ever seen.

"So pretty," Aria breathed as Tatia and Mut dropped their heads.

"You did well, young one of the blood." A woman's voice, pure and sweet, spoke the words inside his head. Jagger glanced at Aria. Her eyes were enormous. This time she heard the voice too.

"Divine One." Tatia dropped to her knees.

The cat sat and licked a paw, twitching one ear.

Divine One? Another goddess. Was it rude to stare? Because Jagger couldn't help himself—the cat was just too glorious.

Aria backed up to his side. She tapped him without taking her eyes off the goddess cat. "I think she's talking to you."

"Uh." He cleared his throat. "Thanks? I guess."

The cat stared up at him, swishing her tail back and forth.

"Um, but, can I ask why?" Jagger couldn't resist the question that had plagued him since this adventure began. "Why me?"

"Why?" Aria whispered with an eye roll. "Of course you did."

The cat stretched luxuriously, then tilted her head to the side before looking directly at Aria then back at Jagger.

"Because you do not walk alone. Because your sister is

beside you. Because the two of you share the blood of your ancestors: your connection to the old families is unique. Because you came here, to Egypt, where the roots of your family's power run deep. Because you two have your own powers, and we believed you would use them wisely. And the powers you possess are wielded by so few—the power of knowledge." She shifted her green eyes to Aria. "And wisdom. My favorite powers in the universe."

She said all this in his head, then stopped, leaving a deafening silence as they all sat stunned, waiting to see if she'd say more. A heartbeat later, the cat eyed the humans one by one, then purred and turned into the night.

"Do animal gods visit you guys all the time?" Aria's eyes were wide like saucers. "That's what she was right? That was no ordinary cat!"

"Isis," Tatia whispered, staring at the empty spot where the cat had just stood.

Jagger shook his head. "But Isis is a cow, or a kite bird. I don't recall her being shown as a cat in this period—"

Tatia ignored him. "I've never heard of a goddess showing herself like that before, except for Meretseger's appearance in the tomb."

"Our gods speak to us, but never directly, never like this," Mut said.

"Okay. A cat," Jagger sighed. He played the words over in his mind. "But what did she mean?"

"She meant what she said, Jagger Jones," the princess stated flatly. "Gods speak only the truth. You were chosen because the gods knew your sister would be by your side. The two of you are descended from our family."

"But what did she mean about their connection to the old gods being unique?" Mut asked.

Tatia shook her head. "I saw nothing to explain that when I cast the *Meseneh Rek.*"

"It helps that the two of you were in Egypt," Mut said, tapping the gold bands that ringed her upper arms. "The spell crosses time, but distance is more complicated, especially when you don't know the person you're trying to bring back. Of course, that's all theoretical. No one has cast the *Meseneh Rek* spell in over two hundred years, until our princess here."

Tatia nodded at Jagger and Aria. "The gods believe you two are knowledgeable and wise. Isis is our most brilliant god—she would recognize those attributes in others."

"There's more going on here than simply saving the family and rescuing Mek's *Ka*," Mut stated thoughtfully. "I don't know why, but the gods are more ... accessible than ever before."

The companions fell silent, lost in their own thoughts.

"Another puzzle for my pile." Mut glanced over at the door. "But now, I must go tell the queen of Mek's passing. She'll want to prepare her along with the little princesses." She blew out a puff of air. "Mek cannot be separated from the amulet. It must stay with her body even as she's embalmed. I'll make sure the king and queen understand so they can tell the priests."

"Wait. Will we see you again?" Aria grabbed Mut's arm. "I mean, we're leaving now. We have to get home to Mom, like … yesterday."

Mut and Tatia exchanged a worried glance.

With a deep, tired sigh, the princess spoke. "*That* is going to be a problem."

SELFIE CARE

"What do you mean?" Aria pulled a stray curl to her mouth.

Jagger shook his head, confused. "We did our part. Now we have to go."

Tatia stared at her feet—she wouldn't look at him. "I said we could send *you* home."

"Yeah." He bit his lip. "So ... what's the problem?"

"*You*," Tatia repeated. She looked up, meeting his eyes.

"Yeah, me. Okay." He stared at her, brain whirling. "Wait, you mean *me*? *Only* me?"

The guilt and misery on her face was all the answer he needed.

The relief he'd carried with him since the moment he knew

Aria was safe vanished, replaced by a sense of betrayal. These people he'd so quickly, and uncharacteristically, trusted had betrayed them. "How can you …? Why didn't you tell us?"

Mut put her hand on Tatia's shoulder, staring down at her perfectly polished toes. Jagger thought back to the cagy way Tatia had spoken about sending them home. She'd known this all along.

"I'm sorry." Tatia dropped down onto the bed. "I should have told you. Aria's arrival was unintended. I hadn't called her. I have no way to send her back."

"Why didn't you tell us?" Aria parroted Jagger's question.

"Because I needed your help," Tatia said flatly, as if the answer justified her treachery. "Saving our family, and Mek's *Ka*, was my priority. I didn't want to do anything that might stop Jagger from helping us. The gods were clear—he was our only hope. Besides, the moment you appeared, it was already too late."

"We thought we might find a solution by the time you returned," Mut added.

Jagger ground his teeth, unmoved by the shame they both wore like a new amulet.

"I'm sorry, Aria Jones." Tatia reached out and grabbed Aria's hand. "I never wanted to hurt you. You'll have an honored place in the palace. This will be your home. You'll be treated like a princess. You'll be like a sister to me. You'll want for nothing."

Aria stared at Tatia if she'd lost her mind. "I'll want my mother. And Grams and Gramps, and my friends, and Dad, and the phone I haven't even got yet. And my future pet dog. I'll want my own country and my own time. I'll probably even want to see my brother again before I die!"

Jagger fell into a cedar chair and wrapped his arms around himself. This couldn't be happening. After all they'd been through, the idea of leaving Aria here was ridiculous. He'd never accept that. There was only one solution. "Send Aria back. I'll stay."

The answer was as obvious as the ivy on the outfield walls of Chicago's North Side baseball field. If only one of them could return, Aria should go back. He'd make peace here somehow. It was an ironic fate for a budding historian, who wanted to read and write about, but never experience, the past. He'd miss Mom and his grandparents, Andrew, and Gino. His sister. Even Dad, if he was honest. He'd miss technology and pizza and feather pillows. Maybe in time they could find a way to send him too.

"You're not hearing me." Tatia shook her head. "I can't send Aria home. I can send you home."

Mut cleared her throat and stepped forward. She looked down at Mek, and some part of Jagger realized this conversation should wait. Tatia had just lost her sister. She should be left alone to mourn before dealing with more BS. But he was too angry to be thoughtful. He'd helped her. Now it was time for her to help him. "Perhaps we should show them," Mut suggested.

Jagger ran his hands over his stubbly head as he watched the princess shrug, then kneel by the bed and pull something out from under it.

"What …" Jagger leaned forward, then pulled back, as repulsed as he was fascinated.

"That's so fierce." Aria dropped to her knees next to the big, shallow, silver dish.

Jagger's face was drawn in the water that filled it. It was like a liquid snapshot, different colors melding into each other to create a remarkably accurate likeness of Jagger's face. How did they do that?

Mut leaned closer. "I've never seen a Horus *cippi* enable such a remarkable likeness. The gods truly are at work here."

Jagger squirmed. "So you're telling me, that because my face is in that bowl of water, and Aria's isn't, you can send me home but not her?"

"Yes, Jagger Jones." Tatia nodded. "The magic requires a likeness. The gods gave me this image. That's how I summoned you. I couldn't have cast the *Meseneh Rek* without it." Her jaw was hard. She looked sad but determined.

In spite of his anger, Jagger felt for her. He'd have done the same in her position. He'd have said whatever needed saying if it meant the difference between Aria enjoying an afterlife and disappearing from existence. But he wasn't ready to let Tatia off the hook yet.

"It's okay." Aria joined Tatia on the bed. "At least Mom will know what happened. I have family here too now. I'll stay. I'll be fine." She gave him a sad smile as the princess hugged her.

"Really, Aria?" Heat crawled up his neck. "You think I'll just reappear after being gone this long, tell Mom you and I had a little out-of-time adventure and that you're going to be an Egyptian princess now so it's all good? You'll be here, and I'll be in some asylum. Or worse!" He knew he was taking his anger out on her, but honestly, what was she thinking? He'd never return without her. She should know that!

Aria dropped her head into her hands and released a giggle that sounded a bit like a sob.

Jagger took a deep breath. No way this was going to stump them, not after all they'd achieved. "Let's breathe." His mind sorted through possibilities. "Wait. Why can't she just touch me? It worked last time."

"It's too dangerous." Tatia's voice was stern. "It's a miracle she made it here alive. There's no guarantee she'd get back in one piece. We can't risk it."

Jagger sighed. "Okay. So ask the gods to make an image of Aria."

"I have," the princess said. "After you left, I used the same Horus *cippi* a dozen times but I can't create an image of your sister. Perhaps the gods want her to stay."

"Your gods aren't in charge of my sister." He slid his hands over his face. Since the moment they got dragged into this insanity, he'd been worried his sister wouldn't survive, that they'd fail to save the princess's *Ka*, that half his descendants would be wiped from history and it'd be his fault. He'd never once worried about getting back, in part because he didn't believe they'd make it this far. But once they'd escaped the tomb with Aria's life and the gemstones, he believed they'd make it home. He'd trusted Tatia and Mut. And they'd just pulled the rug out from under him. "There's gotta be a way," he mumbled. He'd have to think their way out of this one. Tatia and Mut weren't going to do it for him. "Bloody, stupid image," he grumbled.

Image!

He jumped up as the answer hit him. "Wait." He yanked his phone out of his kilt pocket. "Pictures." Jagger pushed the button on his phone, praying to all the gods he could name, modern and ancient, that it would turn on.

"Oh, yeah!" Aria jumped up next to him, smiling. "Duh!"

"Dead!" He groaned. There wasn't even a dash of red bar. He'd used the last of his battery power in the tomb. He had a camera roll full of images of his little sister, useless if he couldn't turn the thing on.

"Okay I'll admit, that blows." Aria folded her arms and glared at him, like this was his fault. "But, I mean, are you a genius or not?" She tapped her toe.

"What do you want me to do? I can't …" He paused, sorting through ideas in his head. "I mean, maybe I could … No. Or …" He slid back onto the chair and closed his eyes. "Okay, this is science," he stammered to himself. "I know this stuff." His eyes flew open and landed on Aria. "Please tell me you still have your change purse."

She dropped to the floor and yanked it out of her bag. "I hope you're not planning to bribe someone. I don't think that would—"

"I need pennies," he interrupted. "Lots of pennies."

She dumped a pile of coins on the plush rug beneath her. A nickel rolled to the painted fish, spun, then toppled over on its head like a new eye. Aria's coins were from countries across the globe, but Jagger spotted pennies everywhere, like bright, little nuggets of gold. Or rather, zinc and copper. And zinc and copper was exactly what they needed.

"We have to charge my phone—"

"What's a phone?" Mut knelt down and ran her fingers over Aria's piles of coins.

Jagger ignored her. "Make two piles of pennies. One pile of pennies from before nineteen eighty-two and another stack of pennies from after." He turned to Tatia. "I need fruit."

"You're hungry?" The princess shook her head.

"No. I'm nerdy," he quipped. "Look." He kneeled down by his sister and stared up at Tatia. "I can get you an image of Aria. A perfect image. Even better than that." He pointed at his watery picture. "But I need fruit. Something strong enough to hold a charge but soft enough to cut," he mumbled. "Dates! And a knife."

"You're going to carve a picture of your sister in fruit? Surely you know that won't—"

"I have her picture in my phone." Their blank stares frustrated him. "I'll show you. Right after you give me some fruit. And ..." He mentally riffled through possibilities. "And I need a file, something to sand hard metal with. Oh, and some of your eye makeup."

Tatia and Mut exchanged a confused glance. The princess nodded, and Mut turned toward the door.

"Wait!" Jagger's stomach dropped. Maybe this solution wouldn't work after all. "How long does the picture have to last?" He could charge the phone, but it wouldn't last long.

"The spell doesn't take long." Tatia shrugged.

"Good." Jagger exhaled. "Because we won't have long."

An hour later, Jagger showed off his contraption. He was as proud as he'd been in second grade when he won the state science fair. Aria found seventy-two pennies from before nineteen eighty-two and even more newer pennies. Mut sanded off the copper plating on one side of the more recent pennies, after shaking her head in confusion at Jagger's explanation that newer pennies had zinc and copper, the two metals needed to create electricity. For good measure, Jagger had Tatia add kohl, which had traces of zinc, as she placed the old and new pennies next to pieces of penny-sized dates and stored them in a tube Jagger rigged from papyrus and leather.

"I'll show you." He pulled out his phone charger—Aria always kept an extra in her purse in case he or Mom needed one—and connected it to the papyrus tube of coins and dates. He pushed the button, willing the phone to spring to life. He sighed as the apple bloomed on his screen. The phone woke up, and he clicked his camera app. "Watch." He pulled Mut into him, and Aria leaned closer, shifting between him and Tatia.

"Ah!" Tatia flinched when the flash flared.

"See." He scrolled to his picture roll and selected the selfie. Though the top of Jagger's head was cut off, enough remained to remind him his hair was too short. Mut and Tatia wore confused expressions, but Aria was perfectly posed, sporting her I'm-too-cute dimples.

"That's impossible," Mut breathed. "How did you …?"

Tatia turned to him and smiled. "I see our family is strong

in magic, even in your time. I do not understand your magic, Jagger Jones. But I like it." Her eyes sparkled.

Jagger and Aria exchanged knowing grins. No need to explain the planet would one day be chuck-full of folks with phones and cameras and GPS systems in their pockets.

He clicked the phone off. "The charge will only last a few minutes. But I have loads of pictures of Aria. So can we go home now?"

"You can take you sister home tonight, Jagger Jones." Tatia's smile was genuine.

25

HOW DO YOU SPELL HOME?

Jagger watched his sister as they rode the carriage toward the limestone cliffs. She chewed her hair, staring into the brilliant, night sky. It looked like diamonds scattered across black silk. "I …" He paused. "Um, I love you, lil' sis."

Aria looked at him and sighed. "I love you too. But do we have to admit it? I'm fine. We can go back to normal now. All this niceness is creeping me out."

He smiled and fell silent. Only the sound of the horse's hoofs punctured the silence of the night. Mut was waiting for them in the tomb, and Tatia sat next to Aria with her eyes shut, emanating a calm Jagger could only dream of. It must be comforting to know you'd see your love ones again, even when they died. People in his time always said the dead were in a better place, but the princess *knew* it.

Fifteen minutes later, the carriage stopped near the limestone cliffs, and Tatia magically maneuvered the large, silver dish that held Jagger's watery likeness toward the tomb. Jagger followed her, clutching the long, papyrus and leather tube, stuffed with pennies and makeup and date slices to his chest, like the fragile treasure it was.

He paused at the top of the same stairs Tatia's voice had led him to in his time. They were clean and tidy now, leading into the desert floor invitingly. The princess walked gracefully down them, followed by Aria, then Jagger. He freed a hand to pat his phone, stuck deep in his pocket, wishing he had more battery to spare so he could light their way. Before he could dismiss the thought, Tatia uttered a word, and a soft light lit the tomb, illuminating the colorful wall art, so faded in their time but brilliant now, even with the dim lighting. A memory struck him, and Jagger moaned, "The light …"

"It's a simple spell." Tatia shrugged. "All magicians learn it early."

Aria rolled her eyes. She was thinking the same thing he was: Herihor could have lit their way anytime. The priest had been working against them in so many ways, and they only trusted him because they were too ignorant to recognize the deceit.

He tried to shake off the sudden anger as he followed his sister through the hallway. She wore her old, leopard striped leggings and pink sneakers. She'd lost the makeup. Her loose curls bounced as she walked, looking like an average, American kid again. But Jagger knew she wasn't the same girl who'd fallen into this tomb a week ago. She'd always been brave, but he'd never considered her wise. Isis's words ran through his head. Had he been wrong about that all along? Or was it new?

He ran his hand over his head, missing his hair more, now that they were headed home. He'd grown used to his head feeling light, but he wasn't sure when the rest of him started feeling lighter too. Maybe acknowledging the anger he'd carted around—anger over his mom's lifestyle choices, his dad's lameness, and his sister's neediness—had set him free.

"Think Mom will be mad?" Aria glanced back at him.

He grimaced. "If she knows we were gone, she's probably been worried sick. She'll just be happy we're okay." His lips shifted into a grin. "Then she'll be mad." He was anxious to see her. He should be used to long stretches away from Mom by now, but this was different—this time he had to worry about her, not just Aria and his grandparents.

Aria stopped and looked back at him. "It's weird how all the travelling we do together made this whole thing easier, huh? It's kinda like we practiced for this." She rushed to catch up to Tatia, leaving Jagger looking after her. *Wisdom!*

"It's ready." Mut stood in the door to the tomb chamber where the boulder had been when they fell into the tomb.

She was dressed in a linen shift studded with gems around the collar and a black wig with blunt bangs, the sides pulled back to reveal large, gold earrings.

"Hemet and Mutef moved that rock," he muttered as the thought struck him.

Aria nodded. "Yeah! Right?"

Mut tilted her head to the side, confused, before shrugging and waving them into the burial chamber.

Jagger's skin felt hot as he walked toward Mek in her sarcophagus, lying with the *ankh* on her belly.

"I'll miss you, Jagger Jones." Tatia put a hand on his shoulder. The other hand sneaked out and pulled Aria close. "And you. But I'm pleased your brother found a way to take you home."

Aria hugged her, one eye on Mek. A wave of sadness hit him as he looked at the younger princess. She wasn't wrapped in her mummy wrappings yet. If he didn't know better, he'd think she was sleeping. The black marks under her eyes had disappeared. The *ankh* sitting on her belly was covered in gemstones that sparkled like trapped fireflies scurried around inside them.

"Are you ready?" Mut touched Jagger gently on the shoulder.

He looked at Aria, who gave him a nod, then turned and threw her arms around the princess's neck again. Mut pulled him into them for a group hug.

When he stepped back, Tatia leaned toward him. "Find your faith, Jagger Jones. Not just faith in yourself, but faith in those you love as well, your sister above all. You've accomplished great deeds here. Take them with you, and push to do more. Start believing. And never stop."

He hung his head, unsure how to respond. He was surprised to realize he'd miss Tatia and Mut. And Babi. Even more surprising, he appreciated this entire adventure. He never thought he'd value being pulled out of his own time and sent on a dangerous trek that almost killed his sister. But the surprising truth was, he did.

"Well," Mut said with an amused gleam in her eye. "Let's get you home."

Tatia joined Mut in front of the sarcophagus. "We need your magic now, Jagger Jones."

He tugged his phone out of his pocket and held his breath as he flipped it on. It worked. He flicked to his camera roll and found an image of Aria. It was one of his favorites, taken on her tenth birthday. They'd gone on a dessert crawl through their favorite South Side restaurants with Mom, Grams, and Gramps, hopping from diner to café to bistro in search of the best dessert on Chicago's South Side. Jagger had snapped the shot just after Aria declared the winner, an especially good tiramisu from one of Chicago's best, Italian restaurants. His sister flashed him a quick grin as he laid his phone down next to his own bizarre likeness.

Mut's eyes pulsed when she saw it. Jagger stood a little taller. He felt proud of impressing these two powerful magicians with his own brand of magic.

"Now what?" he asked, trying to play it cool.

"Stand there." Mut pushed Jagger toward the short end of the painted, cedar chest his image-infused bowl sat on, then directed Aria to the other end of the chest, closer to Jagger's phone.

"You need to hurry," Jagger reminded them. "The charge won't last."

Tatia nodded as she and Mut stood on the opposite sides of the chest with their hands joined over it.

"Hear us, Isis," Tatia began.

"Heed us, Osiris," Mut added.

The wind rose, and the smell of fresh herbs and lotus filled the air. Lights erupted from the sarcophagus, as if the *ankh* had released all its fireflies simultaneously.

"Come to us, Horus," the princess continued.

"Help us, Princess," Mut finished.

"*Meseneh Rek*," they chanted together. "Turn back time."

Mut pulled a papyrus scroll from her robe, unrolling it and handing it to Tatia. The princess's braids whipped in the wind as she pulled out a reed pen and drew two horizontal lines, connected at the ends. It was a simple representation of a mouth, the hieroglyphic version of the letter R. The princess passed the papyrus and reed to Mut, who added a circle with several horizontal lines intersecting it under the mouth. The princess then added a long, vertical rectangle to the right of the other two letters, with a small tie on one side, representing a papyrus role.

"*Rek*," Tatia chanted as she handed the papyrus to Mut, who tied a simple string around it as she added her own "*rek*." With his newfound understanding of ancient Egyptian, Jagger knew the word could mean "time" or "knowledge" or "wisdom."

Tatia smiled at Jagger and Aria, then laid the papyrus on the chest so that it was touching both the bowl of Jagger-looking water and his phone, with Aria's face staring happily up. The wind whipped harder as Jagger looked at Aria across the chest. She was pale. Jagger wondered if she was as nervous as he was. What if something went wrong? What if they didn't make it home after all? Tatia had said something about danger …

The papyrus burst into flames, and Jagger recoiled. The two magicians didn't react. They kept chanting a string of gods' names and titles. The scents and sounds escalated. The wind organized itself, creating a kind of tunnel that sent the lights blowing in the same circular direction. It was like a sparkly whirlwind choreographed to the sounds of the mantra.

Jagger began to feel insubstantial, as if his body wasn't quite real. Instinctively, he reached out for Aria, who must have been experiencing a similar sensation. She reached back.

This was it. He wasn't sure they were going to make it home, but they were about to leave this place. His fingers squeezed Aria's as he searched for Tatia's eyes, hoping for one last goodbye before leaving her behind forever. She was looking over her shoulder, brows furrowed.

Following her gaze, Jagger saw the small, blue *shabti* girl who'd tried to feed Herihor a miniscule fish when they last saw the evil priest in the tomb. She looked … chipped was the word that came to Jagger's mind. A menacing, black smoke whirled behind her, slinking into the room and filling the space, suffocating the dancing lights.

A scream exploded in the room just as Jagger and Aria fell.

Whose scream was it?

Jagger and Aria clung to each other. This time it felt like they were falling up. His phone whizzed past him, and he reached out and grabbed it. The lights still surrounded them, but the black smoke slunk in, tainting the air. The deafening silence they had experienced the first time they fell returned, but it lasted only a moment.

They landed in darkness. The lights vanished the second they hit dirt, and the sound of the wind went with them. Aria's breath boomed through the tomb. Jagger's heart was pounding in his chest.

Jagger clicked on his phone. "The light won't last long."

He looked around. The hiss of Aria's inhaler was loud. They were back where they started, in the tomb, sitting on the ground in front of the sarcophagus, next to the feet of Hemet and Mutef, who were gazing down on them, lit by his phone's dim light. The tomb was dingy and stale again.

"Who screamed?" Aria asked, echoing Jagger's thoughts.

"I don't know." Jagger reached out and touched the cold, gold hand of Hemet, or Mutef perhaps, his mind whirling.

"We have to go back!" Aria tugged at his shirt, as if she could pull him back three thousand years by sheer will alone.

"We can't go back. Not unless they manage to call us again." Jagger took a deep breath, hearing Mom's mantra in his head. "Breathe." Realizing he'd said it out loud, he gave Aria an I'm-sorry-eye-roll. "Think, lil' sis. We're home, just where we wanted to be, just where we worked to get. We can't do anything for them. As close as they feel, the fact is, they lived, and died, thousands of years ago. Right now, we need to find Mom."

Aria scrambled up and tried talking to Hemet and Mutef. They stood silent. Jagger struggled to find some clue in their metallic eyes. Nothing. They simply stared down at him, as if they truly were lifeless.

Aria twirled and leaned over the sarcophagus, rummaging around the mummy.

"Aria!" Jagger wasn't sure why he found her actions so shocking. But now that he knew Mek, or her family at least, it seemed like her mummy should be treated with more respect.

"Got it!" She held the *ankh* up. It was still lit up like a Christmas tree, magical lights sparkling in the dim tomb.

Instinctively, Jagger's hand went to his throat. The Isis Knot amulet was still there. It hadn't crossed his mind to return it to the princess. Clutching it, he thought of Mom.

"She's here," he breathed, surprised the magic still worked. "Mom's close."

"I know," Aria replied with a grin.

Worried as he and Aria both were about their friends, and whatever catastrophe they'd left them in, he could tell she was as excited to see Mom as he was.

Glancing around the tomb one last time, Aria looked at Hemet and Mutef. "We'll be back," she promised, as she tugged Jagger's arm and pulled him toward the exit, sticking the amulet in her purse as she ran toward their mother.

Pronunciation Guide

Amarna – Uh-mar-nuh
Aten – Ah-tun
Akhenaten – Awk-eh-nah-tun
Meretaten – Mare-et-ah-tun
Meketaten – Mek-et-ah-tun
Mutbenret (primarily referred to as Mut, as in "moot point")
– Moot-ben-ret
Mutef – Moo-tef
Hemet – Hem-et
Babi – Bah-bee
Herihor – Hair-ee-hor
Smenkare – Smen-kah-ray
Tutankhamun – Toot-ankh-ah-moon
Nefertiti – Nef-er-tee-tee
Meretseger – Mare-et-say-ger
Seshep ny Netjer (God's Light) – Seh-shep knee net-jer
Heqa-oo Moot (Death Spell) – Heck-a-oo Moot
Meseneh Rek (Turning Time) – Mes-en-eh Wreck
Iroo Herioo (Making Faces) – Ear-oo Hare-ee-oo

Historical Note

The Amarna period was one of the most fascinating periods in human history. Pharaoh Akhenaten truly did move the court to the middle of Egypt and build a new capital on fresh soil. Scholars believe he chose the site because the nearby cliffs mimicked the hieroglyphic symbol for the horizon, which looks like a sun disk rising over two hills. His iconography is unlike anything else in the country's long history. And perhaps most importantly, he elevated the worship of the sun disc, displacing Egypt's traditional gods and goddesses. In fact, Akhenaten is sometimes referred to as history's first monotheist (although he was actually a henotheist: he didn't deny the existence of other gods, he simply claimed the Aten was superior). His advancement of the Aten, a god known but not terribly popular prior to the Amarna period, upended generations of tradition, sending reverberations through all aspects of life including art, architecture, the economy, the military, family life, government, and more.

Many of the characters in the book are based on real people. Akhenaten and his queen, Nefertiti, had six daughters, although I only included five in this story. Meretaten was the oldest, and is well attested, surviving in images scattered throughout museums from London to New York to Cairo.

Meretaten's fate is fuzzy, but her younger sister, the second princess, Meketaten, does seem to have died around this time. She appears to have been memorialized in a chamber of the Royal Tomb of Akhenaten. Two younger princesses may have died around this time as well, possibly from a plague. The third princess, Ankhesenpaaten, survived to marry Tutankhamun, known more widely today as King Tut and famous for his tomb, discovered by Howard Carter in 1922. Smenkare and Tutankhamun are most likely Akhenaten's sons, although Nefertiti is not their mother. The noblewoman, Mutbenret, is similarly attested and sometimes depicted with two companions, Hemetniswernehe and Mutef-Pre (Hemet and Mutef). She's also sometimes shown with Meretaten and Meketaten and may have been Queen Nefertiti's sister. Jagger and Aria are loosely based on my own two, beautiful, biracial children. I'm proud to share my creative, loving little people with the world. I hope they bring my readers a dash of the joy they fill my days with.

I've also included a plethora of historically-attested artifacts, places, and beliefs; indeed, the magic used in this story is inspired by spells and practices that have survived in the archeological record. This series was, in part, inspired by an ancient blessing: *ankh, wedja, seneb*, which means (may you have) life, prosperity, and health. In *JAGGER JONES AND THE MUMMY'S ANKH*, I've tried to contrast how we think about life, *ankh*, with ancient Egyptian notions of life;

thus, the emphasis on the afterworld, a very real, concrete concern for many ancient Egyptians, some of whom, it's worth noting, spent more time and money on the tombs designed to house them for eternity than the homes they spent their lives in. Ancient Egyptians firmly believed that death is forever, while life is fleeting.

But while I used the knowledge I gained earning my Ph.D. in History of the Ancient Near East from the University of Chicago to craft a tale loaded with the spirit of ancient Egypt, I also empowered the storyteller in me to override the historian, which is a complicated way to admit I took liberties with the history currently known to us.

I hope you've enjoyed the history and inspiration behind the adventure as much as I do.

Discussion Questions

1. This series was inspired, in part, by an ancient blessing: *ankh, wedja, seneb*, which means (may you have) life, prosperity, and health. Can you identify differences in how the ancient and modern characters think about "life" in the story? What sections of the story reveal uniquely ancient Egyptian notions and how do they differ from yours?

2. As explored in the book, Pharaoh Akhenaten tried to elevate his favorite god, the Aten, over the many traditional gods of Egypt. Do you think that was good for his country? Can you identify sections of the book that speak to this change and how some ancient Egyptians may have felt about it?

3. Jagger's sense of responsibility is an important theme in the book. "It's your job to take care of your sister," his mother often told him. How does this sense of responsibility manifest itself in the book? How do you think Aria feels about it? Does Jagger change throughout the book?

4. Jagger and Aria have different strengths and they use different resources to solve problems. What are some problems Jagger solved and what personal attributes helped him solve them? What problems did Aria solve and what characteristics enabled her to do so?

5. Jagger is worried about who to trust throughout the book. Do you think he's too suspicious of other people? Do you have a sense of what factors in his life contributed to his struggle to trust people? How does Aria differ from him in this respect? Who do you think is right? Jagger or Aria?

6. Ancient Egyptian artifacts are peppered throughout the book. Can you identify five different artifacts that played an important role in the story? Which ancient artifact was your favorite?

7. If you were trapped in the Amarna period and couldn't get home, what modern luxuries do you think you'd miss most? What would be the best thing about living in ancient Egypt? What do you think would be the hardest thing?

Acknowledgements

I'm not the first gal to amplify the old African proverb: *It takes a village* ... Turns out, the same can be said for publishing a book. Assembling my village has, unexpectedly, turned into one of the most delightful experiences of my life.

The founding member of my village was my son, Gracian, who, at nine years old, bemoaned the fact that the world didn't have a book about a kid who looked like him travelling back to ancient Egypt. *Voilà*—the idea was born. Our village quickly expanded to include my daughter, who inspired a curious, courageous, little sister character. Soren evolved into my most enthusiastic cheerleader and my first beta reader and editor. Our rescue dog, Caesar, was the next sweet soul to wander into our village. Admittedly, his contributions were minor, but his loyalty and constant companionship as I pounded out, edited, and reedited pages earns him a shout-out here.

Soon, the village was augmented by supporters outside our home's walls, starting with Chicago's beloved writing coach, Esther Hershenhorn, without whom I could never have fixed the many problems in my initial draft. I was also lucky for the support of my beta reading friends, Phoebe, Colleen, and Rosaria; my old grad school friends, Jackie and

Solange; and the countless friends and family members who offered support and encouragement.

When the world's greatest agent, Liza Fleissig, joined the leadership team, I knew my village was legit. I was thrilled when Liza pulled my publisher, Georgia McBride, into my orbit. As an unpublished author, finding professionals like Liza and Georgia, who are willing to take a chance on a new writer, is a blessing. I can't thank these two enough for taking my feeble pages and turning them into this magnificent real-life book. There are many things to love about Georgia, but one of those things is that she connected me with Tara Creel, my editor. Tara's patience, creativity, knowledge, and kindness has been a balm, and a blessing. The team at Month9Books has been supportive, engaged, and kind every step of the way, and I extend my appreciation to the entire team: Jennifer, Emily, Nicole, Danielle, Christine, Michelle, and Tom.

And yet, even with all these wonderful villagers, no story is truly launched until it finds an audience. So, my most heartfelt thanks are reserved for readers like you, who pick this book up and, I hope, enjoy the characters, magic, and adventure within.

XO,
Malayna

Malayna Evans

Malayna Evans is the author of a middle grade time travel series—JAGGER JONES AND THE MUMMY'S ANKH is book one in the series. Malayna earned her Ph.D. in Egyptology from the University of Chicago and has used her background to craft a tale loaded with historical details, attested ancient actors, and a magical adventure full of gods, mummies and wriggling creatures. Malayna enjoys a busy life of reading, writing, and playing in Oak Park, Illinois with her two kids, a spoiled rescue dog named Caesar, and a dwarf hamster named Pedicure.

Editor's Note

Dear Reader,

I'm so excited you've picked up a copy of JAGGER JONES AND THE MUMMY'S ANKH. Say that ten times fast, and it may end up sounding like, "JAGGER JONES AND THE MUMMY'S UNCLE!"

When I'm looking for stories to publish, I can never escape my "mommy" hat. I'm always looking for books that my kids or my nieces and nephews might like to read-books they can see themselves in. Where THEY are the heroes and heroines.

JAGGER JONES is a great read for everyone who likes awesome books. Jagger and his sister Aria happen to be biracial, just like my kids. Unlike my kids though, they seem to get along most of the time.

I applaud Malayna for writing such an amazing story, and also wanting to tell it in an authentic way. We all worked really hard to make sure JAGGER JONES, our modern hero, was strong, capable, and unapologetic. This action-packed fantasy adventure is just what the doctor ordered for reluctant readers, advanced readers and kids who love magic. And, between you and I, the author even managed to sprinkle in real historical facts and references, so readers will learn something new as they journey to ancient Egypt with JAGGER JONES.

We hope you enjoy JAGGER JONES AND THE MUMMY'S ANKH.

From our family to yours,

Georgia McBride
Publisher

CONNECT WITH US

Find more books like this at http://www.Month9Books.com

Facebook: www.Facebook.com/Month9Books
Instagram: https://instagram.com/month9books
Twitter: https://twitter.com/Month9Books
Tumblr: http://month9books.tumblr.com/
YouTube: www.youtube.com/user/Month9Books
Georgia McBride Media Group: www.georgiamcbride.com

OTHER MONTH9BOOKS TITLES YOU MIGHT LIKE

METL: THE ANGEL WEAPON

ROGER MANTIS

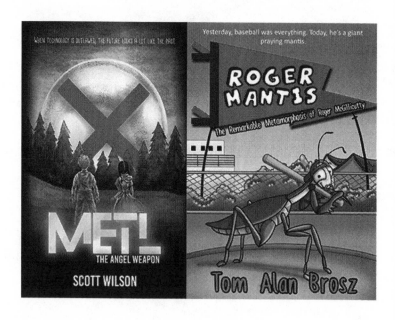